Copyright © 2022 DC Comics & WBEI.
DC LEAGUE OF SUPER-PETS and all related
characters and elements © & ™ DC Comics
and Warner Bros Entertainment Inc. WB SHIELD:
™ & © Warner Bros. Entertainment Inc. (s22)

Published in the United States by Random House Children's Books, a
division of Penguin Random House LLC, 1745 Broadway, New York,
NY 10019, and in Canada by Penguin Random House Canada Limited,
Toronto. Random House and the colophon are registered trademarks
of Penguin Random House LLC.

ISBN 978-0-593-48780-8 (hc) — ISBN 978-0-593-43078-1 (pbk.)
ISBN 978-0-593-43079-8 (ebook)

Printed in the United States of America

10 9 8 7 6 5 4 3 2 1

The Deluxe
Junior Novelization

By David Lewman

Random House 🏠 New York

On the planet Krypton, a white puppy with floppy ears and a big nose scampered across a slippery floor, racing up to a baby boy. SHLURP! The puppy licked the baby's face. Giggling, the boy hugged the pup, and the two tumbled across the floor, having a wonderful time playing together.

"We must hurry," said the boy's father, a scientist named Jor-El. Scooping the baby up and carrying him across his laboratory, Jor-El told his wife, "The planet won't survive a moment longer."

"Are you sure about this?" Lara asked, worried.

"I'm afraid it's the only way," Jor-El assured her, setting the baby in the snug cockpit of a small spaceship. With tears running down her cheeks, Lara caressed her son's face. From the ground, the puppy looked up, confused. "Why are they upset? What is happening?" he thought.

"Krypton is about to die," the scientist explained to his son.

"But you, dear son, will live on," Lara said.

YIP! YIP! The puppy barked at his little friend. He ran toward the spaceship and jumped—

But Jor-El caught the enthusiastic canine in his arms. "Krypto, no!"

The launch sequence began. As the spaceship's glass hatch slowly started to close, the baby boy reached out to the whimpering puppy.

Suddenly, the dog wriggled out of Jor-El's arms and ran toward the ship as fast as his four legs could carry him.

"Krypto!" Jor-El cried.

But Lara held her husband back. "No," she said. "Our boy will need a friend."

Krypto leapt into the spaceship's cockpit, sliding in just before the glass hatch closed. WHOOSH! The ship's thrusters ignited. It launched into space, leaving Krypton moments before the planet began to break into pieces. Staring through the glass at the galaxy whizzing by, the frightened baby began to cry. Krypto licked his face. Soothed, the boy yawned and fell asleep.

Years later, Superman snored loudly in the bedroom

of his Metropolis apartment. ZZZZZ! Krypto, now a full-grown dog, barked at his friend, eager to go on his morning walk.

"All right, buddy," the canine was barking in dog language, "It's walk o' clock!"

Holding his leash in his mouth, Krypto thought, "Maybe I should let him sleep." After about two seconds, he decided, "Okay, time's up!" He jumped onto the bed and climbed on Superman.

But the Man of Steel just kept snoring. ZZZZZ . . .

Krypto pawed at his pal's face, trying to wake him up. He went right on sleeping. The dog gave Superman's jaw a friendly paw-punch. ZZZZZ . . .

"Hmmm," Krypto thought. "All right. You asked for it." He sat on Superman's face. "This is unpleasant for both of us." ZZZZZ . . .

Having no choice, Krypto began wiggling his butt. Muttering "No, no, no . . . ," Superman flipped over, sending Krypto flying off the bed. Sitting on the floor, the white dog cocked his head, determined not to lose this battle. He took the cuff of Superman's pajamas between his teeth and flew into the air above the bed, dangling his friend upside down.

"Five more minutes," Superman mumbled, still half asleep.

Krypto opened his mouth, releasing Superman.

WHUMP! He landed on the floor with a thud.

"And . . . I'm up," Superman said, giving in. "Okay, Krypto—we'll go for a walk."

"Good. You're awake!" Krypto barked happily.

Moments later, high in the sky above Metropolis, Krypto flew through the clouds, dragging Superman, who was still feeling a little sleepy, along behind him by the leash. The Super-Dog and the Super Hero were best friends, always doing amazing things together as a crime-fighting team. Every day was an adventure.

They flew between the gleaming skyscrapers of Metropolis, delighting the workers inside, who gaped through the windows, pointing.

They ran down a gang of bank robbers, bringing them to justice and returning the stolen loot.

They played tug-of-war with Brainiac's arms until the evil robot had no choice but to give up.

They played fetch. When Superman pretended to throw tennis balls and other toys, but hid them behind his back, Krypto used his X-ray vision to find them. Superman wasn't going to fool him that easily!

They spotted a railroad bridge with a gap between the tracks, so they hooked their feet on the ends of the tracks, grabbed each other's hands and paws, and let the train pass over their backs safely. Then they flew into the air and waved at the grateful passengers on the train.

They zoomed over the Atlantic Ocean to Paris, where Superman ordered a warm croissant while Krypto tapped on the glass of the display case with his paw, letting his friend know he'd appreciate one of the delicious French sausages. Or possibly two.

After Krypto had finished devouring his sausages, the two friends flew back to Metropolis and landed in a dog park. Superman was still carrying the croissant in one hand. Holding Krypto's leash in his other hand, he walked over to a park bench and sat next to the reporter Lois Lane, his friend. She had just finished an on-camera report for the TV news.

"Hey, Lois," Superman said, holding up the croissant and winking. "I know you like these, so I got you one from actual Paris." He realized that sounded kind of weird. "I don't know why I said it like that," he added sheepishly.

Krypto noticed that being around Lois made the Man of Steel nervous, but he couldn't figure out why. "Humans!" he thought.

Smiling, Lois held up a hot dog. "And I got you one of these from Forty-Third Street, which is, like, a full three blocks out of my way."

Taking the hot dog, Superman looked impressed.

"During rush hour? Wow, that's like me flying to Mars!" he said.

"What, you can fly?" Lois teased. "I always thought the cape was just a cute accessory."

"Oh, so you think I'm cute?" Superman asked, grinning.

"I said the cape was cute," Lois corrected him.

Superman looked confident. "You think I'm cute."

They leaned toward each other, about to kiss, when—

Krypto jumped onto the bench and sat right between them!

2

"**A**re we licking faces right now?" Krypto asked eagerly. "Because if we're licking faces, I gotta get in on this! There is nothing I like more than licking faces!"

But all Superman and Lois heard was ARF! ARF! ARF! ARF!

Laughing, Superman reached behind his back and grabbed something. "Ooh," he said to Krypto. "What do I have here?" He held a squeaky toy dressed like Batman in front of him.

Immediately, Krypto focused on the toy. "Squeezy Bruce!" Every muscle in his body was ready to run after that toy and fetch it the second Superman threw it. "Don't play, Supes," Krypto barked at his friend.

"FETCH!" Superman shouted, hurling the toy into the air like a rocket.

"Pup up and away!" Krypto cried as he took off, zooming after the toy like a guided missile.

Smiling, Superman turned back to Lois. "Okay," he said, "where were we?" They leaned toward each other again, about to kiss, when—WHOOSH!—Krypto appeared right back between them holding the toy in his mouth.

"Squeezy Bruce retrieved!" he announced proudly, his words muffled by the toy.

Shaking his head, Superman gave a little chuckle at his dog's quick return. "Why don't you go play with those guys over there, buddy?" He hurled the toy across the park toward a pair of dogs.

A Boston terrier was telling a story to a poodle. "So, I'm eating my own vomit, and then—"

SHWOOM! FWOOM! The toy whizzed by, followed closely by Krypto.

Slightly annoyed by this interruption, the Boston terrier repeated, "So, I'm eating my own vomit—"

SHWOOM! FWOOM! The toy and Krypto blasted by the dogs again.

Undaunted, the Boston terrier tried again. "So, I'm eating—"

SHWOOM! BAM! The squeezy toy whipped by a third time. It lodged deep in the trunk of a tree with a ring of flames crackling around the hole for a moment.

"I'm—" the Boston terrier began.

FWOOM! Krypto whooshed in to grab the toy, but

his snout wouldn't fit in the hole, so he easily ripped the entire tree out of the ground!

"And then I said, 'If you don't want me rubbing my butt on the carpet, get hardwood floors,'" the Boston terrier said quickly, finally going on with his story.

With the trunk of the tree in his mouth, Krypto said, "Squeezy Bruce has been retrieved, Super—"

"Wait," the poodle said to the Boston terrier, staring at Krypto. "Do you know who this is? It's Krypto the Super-Dog!"

Krypto dropped the tree and smiled. "Okay," he said, pretending to be reluctant. "You can have my paw-tograph." He dipped his paw in a handy patch of mud and then pressed his paw onto the poodle's face, leaving a muddy print. "Listen—I'm afraid I've got to limit it to just one paw-tograph, or I'll be signing all day. Now if you'll excuse me, I have some pressing hero business." He started to pick up the tree and leave.

Irritated at having his story interrupted so many times, the Boston terrier said, "Hero business? It's just a squeezy toy!"

"Ah, wrong," Krypto corrected. "It's Superman's squeezy toy." He picked up the tree and prepared to fly off.

"He doesn't want it," the poodle pointed out.

Krypto paused. "I'm sorry, what?" he said, the tree still in his mouth.

"Mr. Outside Underpants," the Boston terrier said, meaning Superman. "He doesn't want that squeezy toy. He's just trying to get rid of you. So he can be alone with his girlfriend."

"What!" Krypto said, dropping the tree. "No way! Superman will never love anyone except me!" Feeling confident, he looked across the park at his best friend—and clearly saw him saying "I love you" to Lois!

Krypto's jaw dropped. He suddenly realized how deep Superman's feelings for Lois were. Glimpses of the couple's future together flashed through Krypto's mind. . . .

Superman and Lois are enjoying a romantic dinner together at the dining table. Looking up from the floor, Krypto is horrified to see Lois eating out of his dog bowl!

Lois is opening a gift from Superman—which is a giant bone with a bow tied around it!

Lois is snuggling up to Superman on TV night—taking Krypto's spot on the couch!

Superman is removing Krypto's gold collar and giving it to Lois as a wedding ring!

Superman has married Lois, and the main head-line of the Daily Planet *newspaper announces, "MAN FINDS NEW BEST FRIEND!"*

In reality, of course, none of this had happened . . . yet. Superman and Lois were still sitting on the park bench, kissing. Lois opened one eye and noticed Krypto staring at them. She drew back from Superman and said, "This might sound crazy, but now that we're together, I think Krypto feels left out."

From across the park, Krypto gave them a weird little wave with his paw.

"Yeah," Superman agreed. "I guess I'm his only friend."

"Maybe we can get him a new friend," Lois suggested.

Superman looked intrigued. . . .

3

At a Metropolis animal shelter, a hound named Ace smiled out from his cage. Carl, a friendly deliveryman, walked by carrying supplies. "Good morning, little friends," he said to all the animals in their cages.

Ace's smile disappeared as soon as Carl had passed. "So it begins," he said. "Like clockwork, Carl will try to flirt with Patty."

Sure enough, Carl asked Patty, the owner of the animal shelter, "Did you do something new with your hair?"

"No, I did not!" Patty answered in a chipper voice.

"But Carl will have zero game," Ace observed. He held up his paw. All his claws were cut short except one long one. He planned to use it to pick the lock on his cage. "Giving this handsome canine just enough time to—"

"Whatcha doing, Ace?" interrupted a potbellied pig named PB.

"I'm bustin' loose, PB!" Ace replied in a gruff whisper. He shook his head a little to adjust the blue bandanna he always wore around his neck. "I'm sick of this whole cage situation."

PB was a huge Wonder Woman fan. She'd lined her cage with Wonder Woman comic strips from the *Daily Planet*. Eagerly scanning them, she said, "Oh, my goodness! This is just like when Wonder Woman used her Bracelets of Submission to escape Dr. Poison's secret hideout! Like this!" She tried crossing her arms in a heroic Wonder Woman pose, but her arms were way too short. She ended up tipping over onto her back.

Chip, a nervous squirrel, hid behind his bushy tail. "What if the rescue lady catches you?" he asked Ace frantically. "And locks you in the back room? Where they only listen to smooth jazz?"

"Relax, Chip," Ace told him. "I got my girl, Merton, running lookout."

Merton was an old turtle with blurry vision. "These peepers don't miss a thing," she said confidently. "I am like a hawk, but a turtle. A turtle-hawk."

"Perfect," Ace said, working the lock with his long nail, "because I've almost got myself out of—"

CLINK! Patty slid the latch on Ace's cage shut.

"Oooh, you better be careful, Ace!" she warned. "You almost got out!"

"I think the rescue lady's coming," Merton said way too late.

"Thanks, Merton," Ace said dryly. "Good catch."

PB looked sympathetic. "I'm rooting for you, Ace, but don't you wanna get adopted and feel the warm embrace of a middle-aged person who lives alone?"

"Yeah," Chip agreed, "who will be your new best friend?"

Ace looked as though he couldn't believe what he was hearing. He wasn't waiting around for some human to show up and take him away from his cage. "You're my best friends, dummies," he told the other animals. He got a twinkle in his eye. "And you're all coming with me to the farm."

The farm! Ace had told them about it many times, but they never got tired of hearing about such a wonderful, magical place.

"Oooh, I love when he talks about the farm!" Chip enthused.

Ace got an inspired look on his face. "The farm upstate. An untamed paradise, where animals run free. They love and protect one another. And the lettuce grows on trees."

Merton perked up a little. She was a big lettuce fan.

"No shelter lady watching our every move," Ace continued. "Nope. It's a one-hundred-percent-animal farm!"

"Animal farm," PB echoed dreamily. Although she didn't really have anything against humans, she liked the sound of that.

"It's perfect," Ace concluded. "And when I get us all out of here, that's where we're gonna go."

A hairless guinea pig named Lulu emerged from the shadows of her cage. "The dog is right," she said in a serious voice. "He should seek his freedom."

Ace smiled and nodded. "You see that?" he said. "Lulu gets it."

"And he must destroy all who stand in his way," Lulu said mercilessly, her features curdling into an evil sneer as she stared into a dark future that only she could see. . . .

Ace raised his eyebrows. "Wow! Well, that just took a turn." He'd never really paid much attention to the little guinea pig, but he was starting to think she was much more bloodthirsty than he'd realized.

"You may kid yourself with your silly farm," Lulu scoffed, "but I have the device."

Lulu stepped aside, revealing a strange contraption in the back of her cage. She'd built it herself out of odds and ends she'd found on the floor of the shelter: a hair barrette, a triple-A battery, paper clips, and rubber bands. It was not impressive.

Ace rolled his eyes.

4

Gesturing proudly toward the odd doohickey she'd cobbled together, Lulu continued, "For one day soon, when the stars align, the device will bring me ultimate power, and . . . I WILL BE MORE THAN FREE!"

"You will be more than free," the rest of the animals said at the same time, joining in to repeat what they'd heard Lulu say a million times. They were pretty tired of listening to the guinea pig brag about how she was going to use her device to take over the world someday.

"Exactly," Lulu said, satisfied. She thought that when the other animals chimed in, echoing her words, they were in complete, admiring agreement with her. She never suspected that they were just bored with her outlandish claims.

Ace decided the time had come to set her straight. "Lulu, whatever they tested on you in that lab left you a few guineas short of a pig," he said. They all knew Lulu had been a test animal in a laboratory before they'd come to the animal rescue shelter. "That 'device' of yours is just a pile of junk!"

For just a second, Lulu looked hurt. But then she recovered her confidence. "You fear my brilliance," she said accusingly. "Recede into shadows," she told herself. "Recede into shadows. Maintain eye contact. Recede into shadows." With her eyes narrowed, Lulu backed into the shadowy corner of her cage.

Shrugging, Ace went back to using his sharpened nail to pick the lock on his cage.

Out front, Patty spotted an approaching customer through the window. "Oh, look, Whiskers!" she said excitedly to an orange kitten. "Someone's coming! Act like it happens every day." Curious, Whiskers and a black kitten peered out the window.

Outside, they saw a man tying his dog's leash to a parking meter. The man was Superman—now disguised as Clark Kent, in regular clothes and a pair of black-rimmed glasses—and the dog was Krypto. His cape was hidden inside his plain collar, so he looked like a normal white dog with floppy ears.

"All right, boy," Clark said. "I'll be right back with a surprise."

"And I will remain here, posing under my secret identity," Krypto said, whipping out a pair of his own glasses and putting them on. "BARK KENT!"

He said this loudly to a Corgi tied up nearby, who was so startled, he nearly leapt out of his fur.

"So," Krypto said in a friendly voice, "what is new with you, fellow normal dog?"

The Corgi looked suspicious. Why was this dog wearing glasses? And acting so weird? "Uh," he said, "I bit the mailman the other day."

"Ah, fine job," Krypto said approvingly. "Who was he working for? General Zod? The Legion of Doom?"

"The post office," the Corgi answered, wondering why he'd even ask. Who else would a mailman work for? "What is taking my owner so long?" he said under his breath.

Inside, Patty was showing Clark around the animal rescue center, hoping he'd adopt one of their animals. "So, Mr. Kent," she said, "you're looking for another pet, huh?"

"Well, my dog's the best," Clark said. "But I've got this girlfriend—well, fiancée, actually . . ."

PB overheard him. "Aww," she gushed, charmed by Clark's devotion to his girlfriend.

Lulu didn't share PB's feelings. "Ugh," she sneered.

"Congratulations," Patty chirped.

"Thanks," Clark said. "But my dog doesn't know Lois is my fiancée yet. And I just think maybe he needs a friend of his own."

Patty nodded. "Well, then I think Ace here would be the perfect—"

She turned toward Ace's cage and was dismayed to find it empty. The door was open, swinging slightly on its hinges. Instantly pivoting to a different possibility, Patty said, "How do you feel about guinea pigs?"

Ace had made his way to an open window and was climbing out. "I'll come back for all of you guys after closing!" he called back to his friends. "Stay strong!"

The hound squirmed through the window and dropped down into the alley behind the animal rescue center. He turned toward the street. Freedom!

Hurrying down the alley, Ace was about to step from the shaded passageway onto the brightly lit sidewalk when Krypto blocked his path.

"Hold up!" Krypto ordered, raising a paw. "I'm afraid I can't let you pass." He'd smacked the tag on his collar, revealing the *S* (for Super-Dog) and releasing his red cape. It fluttered in the breeze.

Ace scowled. "I don't have time for this Super-Dog mess."

"I'm sorry," Krypto explained, "but as a hero, it's my duty to protect you. The streets are a very dangerous place for a dog without an owner."

Ace made a face. "An owner? *Pfft*. I never had an owner. Never wanted one, either. I'm a wild animal. Can you own the wind? Can you? What about a dream? Can you own that?"

Krypto was thrown. He'd never heard a dog talk this way before. "Well," he answered, "I have an owner, and he's kinda the best."

"Congratulations," Ace said. "Now get outta my way!"

Ace tried to run past Krypto on his right, but Krypto shifted in front of him. Ace tried to pass him on the left, but Krypto blocked him on that side, too. Then Krypto calmly used his freeze breath to trap Ace's paws in a block of ice.

"That's cold, man," Ace said.

Inside the rescue center, Clark leaned over and peered into Lulu's cage. She glared at him. "Aren't you a little ray of sunshine?" he said, smiling.

Outside, he heard some kind of commotion. Using his X-ray vision, Clark looked right through the wall into the alley. He saw Krypto barking at Ace and sighed. "Ah, Krypto," he said to himself.

Lulu noticed what Clark was doing and was intrigued.

In the alley, Ace shook his paws one by one, freeing himself from the chunk of ice. But Krypto immediately used his heat vision to melt the ice into a puddle. Trying to run off, Ace kept slipping in the puddle. "Stupid Super-Dog," he muttered as he struggled to regain his footing.

Finally, just as Ace was about to take off, Carl snatched him up from behind. "Gotcha!"

Ace tried to get free, but Carl held him tight in his arms and carried him back into the animal rescue shelter. Ace looked back at Krypto and said very sarcastically, "Thanks a lot, weirdo."

"You're welcome," Krypto answered sincerely.

Carl carried Ace back to his cage, put him inside, closed the door, and put an extra lock on the door. "Nice try, Houdini," Carl said, referring to the magician who was famous for his amazing escapes.

As Carl walked away, Merton said to Ace, "Well, you did say you'd come back for us."

A cute little girl walked into the room with all the cages.

"Ooh, adoption time!" PB squealed. "One of us is going to get someone to snuggle with."

"Don't get your hopes up," Ace warned. "They always pick the kit—"

"Here you go, baby!" Patty said, handing the girl the black kitten who'd peered out the window with Whiskers.

"Wow, first day!" the black kitten exclaimed. "Being a rescue animal is easy and fun!"

The little girl hugged the adorable kitten and

happily carried her out of the animal rescue center. The kitten waved goodbye with her tiny paw.

"See?" Ace sighed. "People love kittens. And honestly, I get it. Sweet little purr-purr babies—that's what I call 'em." He noticed PB looking sad and discouraged. "Hey," he assured her, "you'll get 'em next time."

"Yeah," PB said in a small, unconvinced voice. "Next time."

Back in Superman's apartment, Krypto was saying to himself, "I can't believe that dog called me a weirdo." Hovering over the toilet in the bathroom, Krypto finished his business and flushed. Then he washed his paws in the sink and checked his teeth in the mirror for any unsightly bits of food.

In the living room, Superman sat on the couch reading a book called Socializing Your Dog. Krypto flew in from the bathroom, did three circles in the air over his dog bed, and then settled down onto it. He pulled out a copy of the long Russian novel *War and Peace* and pretended to read it. Unfortunately, he was holding it upside down, so he failed to fool his friend.

"Sooooooo," Superman said with a sigh. "We had a little setback at the shelter. You're clearly not great with other animals. But that's all right. We can practice!" Before he could get down on all fours like a dog, there was a loud rumble outside. The two friends snapped to attention.

"What's that?" Superman asked.

"What's that?" Krypto barked.

They rushed to the window and were horrified to see a giant Kryptonite meteor hurtling through the sky, straight toward Metropolis! Kryptonite—Superman's only weakness!

"Someone is dragging a meteor toward the city!" Superman said. Krypto barked the exact same thing.

Sure enough, a powerful magnetic beam was hauling the space rock toward LexCorp Tower. "Luthor!" Superman exclaimed.

Krypto growled. . . .

On a rooftop deck atop LexCorp Tower, Super-Villain Lex Luthor operated a tractor beam, pulling in the glowing meteor. "Hello, gorgeous," he said, grinning at the approaching meteor. "Oh, how I have longed for you to enter my solar system!"

He turned toward his longtime assistant, Mercy Graves, to see how impressed she was by this accomplishment. She shrugged. "It's a rock."

Luthor scowled. "That rock is one hundred percent Orange Kryptonite."

Mercy wasn't impressed. She'd seen Luthor try and fail to beat Superman with Kryptonite many times. "Cool. Another Kryptonite scheme."

"No, this one's different!" Luthor snapped. "Green Kryptonite takes away Superman's powers. But Orange Kryptonite will give me powers. You know, like invisibility! Or laser eyes! Or throwing playing cards really hard!" He smiled, thinking about having superpowers. "I'm finally gonna be stronger than that—"

"You're not talking about me, are you?" Superman interrupted.

Krypto barked.

"Yup," Superman agreed. "I think he was talking about me, too. That's awkward."

The two were hovering in the air right by the edge of the rooftop deck.

"Superman," Luthor said, turning to face his foe. "I expected you and that mutt of yours much sooner."

Krypto snarled. He didn't like Lex Luthor one bit.

And he didn't appreciate being called a mutt.

"I'm gonna need you to let go of that meteor, Lex," Superman said, calmly but firmly.

Luthor grinned an evil grin. "Gladly," he snarled. He clicked off the tractor beam, and the giant boulder hurtled toward the citizens of Metropolis!

"Krypto, fetch!" Superman cried as they flew down after the falling meteor.

Narrowing his eyes, Krypto raced ahead with his jaws open wide. Just as the meteor was about to hit the ground . . . CHOMP! Krypto clamped his jaws shut on the huge rock and hit the brakes, stopping just before he and the rock reached the pavement. He lifted the rock, holding it aloft.

"Good boy!" Superman called to him. He flew down and landed near his pup. "Any Kryptonite on Earth is dangerous. Let's put this thing back in space, where it belongs." He got under the meteor near an awestruck mother and her newborn baby. He gave them a little salute. "Ma'am. Baby."

Grabbing onto the meteor, Superman zoomed up into the air with Krypto in tow. But just as they were about to hurl the rock into space—FWOOM!— Luthor's tractor beam slammed into them both, knocking the Orange Kryptonite meteor out of their grasp. The space rock was sent plummeting back down toward the citizens of Metropolis.

The two Super Heroes were trapped in the beam.

"Let's see if you can catch it now!" Luthor gloated.

6

Luthor grinned maniacally, sure the meteor would smash into the city this time. But even though the Man of Steel couldn't fly down to catch it, Superman didn't look worried.

WHOOSH! From the shore of a nearby river, Aquaman appeared, creating a massive wave of water that caught the meteor!

"You forgot one thing, Lex," Superman said, smiling. "Unlike you, I have friends."

Aquaman waved to Luthor, calling, "Thanks for building your evil headquarters on the river! Very convenient for the water guy! I'm Aquaman!"

Jealous about having to share Superman's attention with other members of the Justice League, Krypto sighed. "Oh, great. These guys."

As Luthor frowned, Cyborg—a man named Victor Stone with an advanced cybernetic body—flew in behind him. "Did somebody call tech support?" he said. "Have you tried turning it off and turning it back on again?"

ZZZWORP! Cyborg zapped the tractor beam with a blast of energy, knocking it out and freeing Superman and Krypto.

"Thanks, Vic!" Superman called gratefully.

But Krypto shook his head, telling Cyborg, "You know, me and Supes were totally handling this ourselves!"

More help from the Justice League was on the way. Wonder Woman flew by in her Invisible Jet and whisked up Superman and Krypto. "Please fasten your seat belts," the Amazonian princess asked them politely. "They are invisible."

Superman smiled. Krypto frowned.

"Yeah . . . none of this stuff is invisible," Krypto pointed out. "It's really more transparent."

ZARP! ZWAP! ZWACK! Mercy fired at the Invisible Jet with Luthor's laser cannon!

But then—FLICK!—a giant glowing green hand flicked Mercy away from the cannon. The hand had emerged from the green ring worn by another member of the Justice League: Jessica Cruz, better known as Green Lantern!

"I like your laser thing," Green Lantern said, referring to Luthor's laser cannon. "But I like it better in green." She used her powerful green ring to create a glowing copy of the cannon.

Frustrated by these setbacks, Lex Luthor pressed a button, instantly armoring himself in a big mechanical suit. "LexCorp power suit engaged," the suit announced.

"Best billion I ever spent," Luthor said, full of self-satisfaction. "Look at this thing. It's titanium." Blasting up into the air, he flew off the rooftop and after the meteor.

But before he could reach it, Superman and Krypto dove off Wonder Woman's Invisible Jet and grabbed hold of the Orange Kryptonite boulder. They flew straight toward the stratosphere, preparing to hurl the rock into space.

ZHWOOOOK! Luthor fired his power suit's arm laser right at the rock. BLAM! Pieces of the meteor broke off and fell toward Earth. "All I need is one little piece," he said, grinning. Speeding through the air in this power suit, he dove down to catch one of the Kryptonite fragments. He'd almost reached it when The Flash zipped up beside him.

"Oh, bless your little heart," The Flash said. "Did you think you were going to get to that piece before me?" The speediest member of the Justice League snatched the rock out of the air and disappeared in a red blur.

Down below, citizens saw the falling meteors and ran to take cover. But before the pieces could hit the ground, The Flash quickly gathered them, one by one. WHOOSH! WHOOSH! WHOOSH! After he'd caught the last fragment, he skillfully juggled them, whistling a happy tune.

ZOOM! Krypto flew by, grabbing all the meteors in his mouth. "Thank you!" he told The Flash with his mouth full. Then he zipped back up to Superman so they could hurl the pieces into space.

CLACK! Luthor's power suit hand flew up and snatched one tiny meteorite. Back on the roof of Lex-Corp Tower, Luthor deactivated his suit and held the glowing orange pebble in his hands, its light shining off his face. With an evil laugh, he crowed, "I AM TO BECOME WHAT I WAS ALWAYS MEANT TO BECOME!"

Holding the meteorite tight, he raised one fist in the air and jumped, ready to fly. WHOMP! He face-planted on the deck. He opened his hand to look at the glowing orange rock. He tried using his superpowers—lifting a heavy cannon, firing a heat ray from his eyes, blowing a freezing blast of cold air—but nothing happened. "What is this?" he cried. "I'm supposed to have superpowers!"

BAM! Batman tackled Luthor. "Superpowers are overrated," he said.

Batman's tackle knocked the meteorite out of Luthor's hand. It tumbled over the edge of the roof and fell toward the ground . . .

. . . only to be caught by Krypto and thrown into space!

"Good boy, Krypto!" Superman said, petting his friend. "Who's a good boy? Who's a good boy? Are you my doggo? Are you my super doggo? Oh, who's a good boy?" Krypto showered his pal with happy licks.

The members of the Justice League didn't understand Superman's love for his dog.

"I've seen some genuinely disturbing things in my life," Batman said, "and this is right up there." The others nodded in agreement, except for Aquaman.

"What?" he said. "I kiss my fish on the lips all the time."

"We know," Wonder Woman and Green Lantern said together, rolling their eyes.

"Little fishy kisses," Aquaman said cheerfully.

"Who threw that Kryptonite back into space?" Superman was saying to his beloved dog. "Krypto did!"

But at the very moment Superman was praising Krypto for launching the meteorite into the depths of outer space, the Orange Kryptonite fragment was freezing in place, caught by a tiny tractor beam.

Lulu's tractor beam.

In her cage at the animal rescue center, Lulu worked the controls of her device. What had seemed like junk was all lit up, looking much more impressive than it had before. The guinea pig stared out the window at the sky above as she pulled the Orange Kryptonite shard closer and closer. "Hello, gorgeous," she said, grinning. "Oh, how I've longed for you to enter my solar system." Without knowing it, she was using the exact same words Lex Luthor had uttered.

Ace rolled his eyes.

As Merton slowly inched toward a piece of iceberg lettuce, the tiny Orange Kryptonite piece smashed through the window, bounced off Lulu's cage, and slammed to the floor. A tiny part of it broke off, which knocked into Merton's lettuce, sending it flying through the bars of her cage and out of her reach.

"You win this round, lettuce," Merton sighed.

SHOOYOOOYOOYYOOYOOM! An orange radioactive wave rippled out from the tiny rock, catching the animals in its glow. They squinted at the shining rock, astonished.

7

"**G**uys, what's going on?" PB asked, bewildered.

Lulu stared at them with a menacing look on her little guinea pig face. "Nothing, PB," she said. "It's just that the plan you all called crazy turns out to be crazy good!"

She pulled a tag out of her device and it powered down, returning to appear to be nothing more than a pile of scraps and bits of trash. The microchip tag had been her ID when she was an experimental subject at a laboratory. It read LU1V. She clipped the tag back onto her ear. The back of the tag read LEXCORP. Lulu had been a lab animal for Lex Luthor!

The other animals weren't impressed by Lulu's claim that her plan had been proved to be crazy good. They just rolled their eyes, used to her grandiose bragging.

"You see," she continued, "back in the lab, there was this human, Lex." She smiled, remembering the first time Lex Luthor had leaned over and grinned into her cage. "Together we were two scientists searching for ultimate power. Of course, there were missteps along the way."

Lulu was lost in thought, recalling all the different kinds of Kryptonite Luthor had stuck into her cage to see what would happen. "The Red Kryptonite made my hair fall out," she explained.

"Oh," PB thought, "so that's why Lulu doesn't have any hair. . . ."

"Purple Kryptonite gave me uncomfortably vivid dreams," she continued. "But the Orange . . . we knew the Orange Kryptonite would be different. Lex tracked the Orange Kryptonite on his computer, analyzing its makeup."

"It wore makeup?" PB asked, confused.

Lulu ignored her question. "And we had a plan, until Krypto the Super-Dog had to burst into the lab and ruin it. Krypto . . . what a stupid name. Named after his planet. Oh, real creative. Like naming your baby Eartho."

"Eartho," PB echoed. "That's a pretty name!"

"What did Krypto do?" Chip asked.

Lulu frowned. "Oh, he used his stupid heat vision to melt all the locks on the cages, setting all the other guinea pigs free. They thanked him and ran off, but I stayed in my cage, refusing to go. 'What the heck are you doing?' I asked him. 'I'm freeing you from

41

this horrible animal-testing lab!' he claimed. Then he picked me up in his awful, drooly mouth!"

She shuddered, remembering. "I told him, 'No! This is my home!' but he wouldn't listen to me. He carried me straight to this animal shelter and set me down. He said, 'And now this is your new home! You're welcome!'"

"How long is this story?" Merton asked. "I mean, we turtles live a long time, but not forever."

Lulu ignored that question, too. "The shelter lady—"

"Patty," Ace said helpfully.

"WHATEVER!" Lulu roared. "She picked me up, saying, 'Oh, you're the sweetest.' I told her in no uncertain terms, 'Unhand me!' But she put me in this cage and locked the door."

The others nodded. Each of them remembered the moment when they'd been put in a cage and the door had been locked.

"So, I bided my time in this disturbing hovel," Lulu said. "Preparing. Collecting the parts I needed for the device. A battery from a remote control. A barrette from a little girl."

"Ooh, that's stealing," Chip said reproachfully.

Lulu got a triumphant look on her hairless face. "Because I knew something that even Lex didn't.

Orange Kryptonite doesn't work on people. It only works on PETS!"

Grinning, Lulu stared at the lock on her cage, concentrating. Her head glowed orange! Then . . . SHING! The catch slid open! Lulu could move things with her mind!

"Uh, Lulu?" PB said, concerned. "Are you okay?"

Using only her brain, Lulu made her cage door swing open. Then she stepped out . . . FLOATING ON AIR!

"Oh, I'm more than okay, pig," she gloated. "I am what I was always meant to become!" With a tiny flick of her guinea pig wrist, she sent a metal chair flying across the room without even touching it. CRASH! The chair smashed into a computer monitor, setting off sparks.

The display of power made Ace a little nervous. But he was also impressed, and quickly realized it might be a way out. "Lulu, hey, take us with you. Us shelter animals, we gotta stick together, right? Solidarity!"

"Oh, Ace, I'm sorry," Lulu said sarcastically. "I don't really have time in my life right now to take care of a PET!" WHAM! Lulu hurled debris at Ace's cage. With little waves of her paw, she sent everything that wasn't nailed down flying across the room. Her

43

last gesture caused a fire to ignite! With the Orange Kryptonite in tow, Lulu floated toward the exit.

"Lulu, wait!" Ace shouted as the flames spread. "Do NOT leave us here!"

"Don't worry," she assured him. "I'm sure someone wonderful will adopt you any day!"

"What about me?" asked Whiskers, the adorable kitten. "Will you take me?"

"Oh, of course," Lulu said sincerely. "I'm not a monster." With a flick of her paw, she freed Whiskers and took her along.

"Wow!" Whiskers exclaimed. "First day!"

As they left, Lulu turned back and said, "Miss you, love you! Have fun!"

The flames rose, drawing closer to the rescue animals' cages. PB screamed in terror.

"Hold on, PB!" Ace yelled. "I'm gonna get us out!" He desperately slammed against his cage door, but it held tight.

Now the flames were very close to PB's cage. She tried to squeeze through the bars, but she was too big. Too scared to watch the fire, she closed her eyes, wincing. But then she began to glow orange and shrink until she was only three inches tall! She easily slipped through the bars to safety! When she opened her eyes, she looked at herself and squeaked, "Guys, I'm small!"

"What just happened?" Merton said, rubbing her eyes. "No, seriously, what just happened? I can't see worth a darn."

"The Orange Kryptonite gave me powers, too!" PB said in a high voice. "This is my origin story! And my uncle didn't even have to die!" she added.

But the fire was still burning, approaching dangerously close to Ace, weakening a beam in the ceiling right above him. "Yeah, that's great," he told PB, "but it isn't looking too good for your old pal Ace."

8

PB squeaked, "Wonder Pig—still working on the name—is on it!" She rushed to the rescue, but realized she was too small to reach anything. "Uh-oh," PB said in her tiny voice.

CRASH! The ceiling beam gave way, falling right on Ace's cage and crushing it!

"ACE!" Chip screamed.

"Ace, no!" PB cried.

All the animals stared at the smashed cage, heartbroken. But then . . .

KA-POW! Ace punched his way out of the mangled pile, alive and uninjured! His body was glowing orange. "I should be a lot more dead right now, right?" he said, puzzled.

"Oh my gosh!" PB exclaimed. "The Orange Kryptonite gave *you* powers, too!"

Chip looked thrilled. "You're super-strong! And your tail is now made of fire!"

"My what is what?" Ace asked. He looked around

and saw that his tail was indeed on fire. He quickly blew out the flame.

"No," PB corrected. "You're invulnerable! And I can shrink myself down to the size of a . . ."

WHOOMP! PB instantly grew until she was twenty feet tall! Her head crashed through the ceiling into the apartment above the shelter. The upstairs neighbor was right in the middle of a bubble bath. Embarrassed, PB forced a smile and said, "Still working out the kinks. I didn't see anything."

She shrank back down to normal size, ready to help Ace save the others from the fire. "You go get Chip!" Ace told her. "I'll get Mert!"

As PB trotted toward Chip's cage, Ace rushed to Merton's. The old turtle was desperately pushing against the bars. The heroic hound leapt through the flames and ripped off the cage door. WHOOSH! Merton shot out of the cage at lightning speed on her glowing-orange feet, leaving a trail of flames behind!

A second later, she zipped back to chomp on the piece of lettuce that had gotten away from her earlier. "In your face, lettuce!" she cried triumphantly.

As a ceiling fan fell toward him, Chip shivered in his cage, his eyes shut tight, screaming, "AAAAHHH!" Just in time, PB tore off his cage door and snatched Chip to safety. As debris crashed around the two of them, they all dashed into a back room.

Disappointed, Chip said, "Great, I'm the only one who didn't get any superpow—" Lightning bolts shot out of his glowing-orange claws. Startled by this sudden burst of energy, Chip screamed. "YAAAHH-HHH!"

"Come on, let's get out of here!" Ace urged as sirens sounded and the sprinkler system turned on.

"Right!" Merton agreed. She zipped off down the hallway. WHAM! She slammed into a wall. "Update," she said. "I'm fast now, but I still can't see worth a darn."

The newly empowered friends ran off together.

That night in Superman's apartment, Krypto took popcorn out of the microwave oven. "All right!" he said happily. "Thursday night! TV night. Time for my favorite show with the best friend in the whole wide—"

Krypto noticed Superman dressed as Clark Kent, checking himself out in the mirror. He used his heat vision to steam the wrinkles out of his shirt.

"Oh, look at you, all spiffy," Krypto barked. "Pretty dressed up for watching our baking show. But you know what? It makes sense. This is the season finale."

BZZZZ! The front door buzzer sounded. On the video feed from downstairs, Krypto saw Lois waiting in the lobby.

"You have a date?" he said, hurt. "On baking show night?"

Krypto imagined zipping down to the lobby, grabbing Lois by the heel of her shoe, and flinging her out of the building. But he knew that wasn't a good idea.

Superman pushed the call button by the video screen. "Hey, Lois!" Then he caught sight of Krypto, standing by a bowl of freshly popped popcorn, glaring at him. He could tell his Super-Dog was one upset pet.

"Oh," Superman said hesitantly. "Listen, buddy . . ."

Krypto flew to block Superman's path to the apartment door. "This is Pie Week!" he reminded the Man of Steel forcefully, hovering in the air. "Your choice. Her or me."

Superman nudged his dog aside. Krypto growled.

Superman looked surprised. He'd never seen Krypto behave like this. "What's gotten into you?" he said sternly. "Bad dog!"

Krypto stared at Superman, stunned. He couldn't believe what he'd just heard.

9

"**W**hat did you just call me?" Krypto barked. "That is way out of line, fella." He was still floating in midair, blocking the door. Superman moved him out of the way. As he headed out, he turned back and told his dog, "We'll talk about this when I get home."

He closed the door behind him. Krypto's head drooped. He felt heartbroken.

But then the door opened! Krypto perked up! Superman had come back! He must have realized the error of his ways. You can't just walk out on a season finale!

"I missed you so much!" Krypto gushed.

But Superman just tossed a dog toy through the open door, explaining. "You left Squeezy Bruce in the hallway again." He looked at Krypto sheepishly, feeling a little guilty about leaving him.

Krypto stared at him defiantly. "Fine! I'll watch the crusts crisp alone!" As Superman pulled the door closed again, Krypto called, "Bad owner!"

All by himself in the apartment, Krypto headed for the bedroom, sulking. He left the squeaky Batman toy on the floor near the apartment door.

He hopped onto the bed, turned on the TV with the remote, and pulled on a pair of noise-canceling headphones. He cranked up the volume on a pop song. Krypto watched the baking show for the visuals, not the commentary. While looking at the TV, he reached down to the floor for one of Superman's boots. Bringing it to his mouth, he started chewing on it. He hadn't really chewed on shoes since he was a puppy, but in his current mood, it just felt right.

As Superman started down the hallway, eager for his date with Lois, but a little worried about Krypto, he heard a strange sound. It was a combination of high-pitched squeaks and grunts.

"Huh?" he said.

He looked down and saw Lulu staring at him with fire in her little guinea pig eyes.

"Kal-El, son of Jor-El," she said, using the name he'd been given back on Krypton, "I am Lulu. Daughter of Cinnamon. And you will kneel before me!"

Superman understood none of this. All he heard were cute little guinea pig noises. "Wait a minute," he said. "Aren't you the hamster from the shelter?"

"I am a guinea pig," Lulu corrected him. "And I said KNEEL!" She reached behind her back and pulled out a shard of Green Kryptonite, holding it up toward Superman! He staggered, his powers beginning to get sucked away by the green crystal. He crashed against his apartment door and collapsed to the floor.

"Well, looky-looky what I got from the old lab," Lulu said waving the Green Kryptonite in his direction.

Trying to gather his remaining strength, Superman called weakly to his loyal friend. "Help," he said. "Krypto . . ."

But Krypto still had the headphones on, blasting his favorite song at full volume, singing along as he watched the baking competition on TV. He only paused in his singing to gnaw a little more on Superman's red boot.

In the hallway, Superman grew woozy, close to passing out, as the energy drained from his body. "You really should have made it harder to find you," Lulu told him. "Those glasses aren't fooling anyone. Mustache, maybe, but not glasses." Using the power given to her by the Orange Kryptonite, she gestured with her paw, causing Superman's Clark Kent disguise glasses to fly off his face and smash into the wall. Then she used her power to tear off his Clark Kent clothes, revealing the Superman outfit underneath.

Superman knew he was in serious trouble. This bald hamster meant business!

Outside the apartment building, Lois had just arrived at the front door, ready to meet Clark for their date. CRASH! She looked up and saw Superman smashing through the roof of the building as though he was being propelled by some unseen force. He wasn't flying—he looked unconscious.

"Well, there's tonight's lead story," Lois said. She pulled out her phone and quickly called the number for the Justice League's hotline.

A recorded voice answered. "You've reached the Justice League emergency line. For bank robberies, press one. For an interdimensional demon, press two. For an escape from the Phantom Zone—"

Lois heaved a heavy sigh.

Hovering in the air above Superman's apartment building, Lulu laughed. "Oh, man," she said, "that looked like it hurt! I hope it did!"

Summoning every last drop of his waning strength,

Superman managed to kick the Green Kryptonite fragment out of Lulu's paws. The glowing stone fell over the side of the roof and down to the pavement below, where it skidded across the sidewalk and fell through a sewer grate.

Still dazed but already feeling better, Superman drew himself up, facing Lulu as they both hovered over the roof.

"Wow, look at you still trying," Lulu said sarcastically. "Plucky. Fine, then. Mama likes a good fight." She gave him a little "come and get it" gesture with her paws.

Superman rushed at Lulu, and the battle between the Man of Steel and the Pig of Guinea was on! Lulu was not an opponent to underestimate, since the Orange Kryptonite had given her the power to move even the biggest object with a wave of her paw. Though Superman was still at low power from the draining effect of the Green Kryptonite, he remained a Super Hero with years of fighting experience. He managed to corner Lulu and grab her in a tight grip.

"Surrender!" he said. "I don't want to hurt you!"

"No, no, no!" Lulu cried. But then . . .

. . . she triumphantly brandished the shard of Green Kryptonite! Lulu had reached out with her amazing power and pulled the shard out of the sewer, bringing it all the way to her little guinea pig hand.

"AGH!" Superman gasped, feeling his superpowers strength slip away again.

"A little advice," Lulu said, grinning as she taunted her defeated foe. "Never test a guinea pig, mm-kay?"

10

Back in Superman's apartment, Krypto headed from
the bedroom to the kitchen for a snack. When he saw
the Batman squeak toy on the floor near the door, he
paused. "I can't believe he really left with her," he said.
"They're probably out there playing fetch together as
I speak!"

Disgusted at the thought of Superman's disloyalty,
Krypto slapped the toy away with his paw. With a high-
pitched squeak, it slid across the floor and smacked
into a wall.

A tiny chunk of cheese fell out of the toy.

"Oooh!" Krypto said, excited. "He left me cheese!"

He scampered across the room and gobbled up the
little cheese chunk. "I can't stay mad at the guy," he
admitted after he'd swallowed the delicious cheese.

Through an open window, Krypto heard a familiar
voice calling weakly, "Help . . . help . . ."

"Superman!" Krypto cried, racing to the window.

He peered out and saw Lulu using her Orange Kryptonite powers to drag Superman away on the street below. Narrowing his eyes, Krypto reared back, determined to save his friend.

"Pup, pup, and awaaa—"

He jumped out the window and immediately plummeted to the ground below, landing with a painful crunch! "OOF!" he cried. Then he let out a groan. "Ohhhh . . ."

Superman was watching from across the street. He turned to Lulu. "What have you done to him?"

"I'm not super anymore," Krypto moaned. "Why? What happened to me?"

Lulu stopped dragging Superman for a moment and turned around to talk to him. "I see someone found his medicine," she said with a smirk. "A tiny shard of Green Kryptonite cleverly concealed in a hunk of Swiss cheese—by me!" She happily continued on her way, pulling Superman behind her, disappearing down an alley.

"They always put it in the cheese," Krypto wheezed as he struggled to his feet and staggered after his friend and the villainous guinea pig.

In the alley, Lulu used her powers to rip a piece of Superman's cape off and fasten it around her own neck as a mini cape. She tucked the shard of Orange Kryptonite inside the band of fabric. Then she called back to Krypto, "You took me away from Lex, so now I'm taking Superman away from you. Oh, and don't worry—your powers will be back in a few days, months, or centuries. I don't know. The science is still out on this one."

"Must protect Superman," Krypto gasped, trying hard to follow Lulu.

Still weak and hurt by his fall, he collapsed into a pile of dirty trash bags and promptly passed out.

Later that night, Krypto came to in the trash pile. Blinking, he looked around, but Superman was nowhere to be seen.

"Superman! I have to find him!" he said. But when he tried to stand up, pain shot through his body. Without his superpowers, he felt pain just like a normal dog. "I should have been there to save him," he admitted to himself sadly. "But I was watching a baking show. I am a bad dog."

No sooner had those self-accusing words come out of his mouth than the tag on his collar opened up. A black-and-white hologram was projected into the night sky. He saw a dog who resembled himself, only older, wearing some kind of alien cloak. "Father?" Krypto said.

"Yes, it is I, Dog-El," the hologrammatic dog said solemnly. "When you were just a puppy, I recorded all my knowledge in your collar."

"Yes," Krypto said a little impatiently. "You've appeared to me, like, a thousand times. Back on the farm in Smallville; last Tuesday, when I lost that bone . . ."

"I am your father," the dog in the hologram said.

"I know," Krypto sighed. "And this time I could really use your help."

"Indeed," Dog-El agreed. "You look like hot garbage."

Krypto nodded sadly. "Yeah, I lost my powers. I'm not a hero anymore."

Dog-El shook his head. "It's not superpowers that make you a hero, Krypto."

"Then what is it?" Krypto asked curiously.

"I'm just a hologram," Dog-El reminded him. "You're lucky I know this much!" His voice became heavy with emotion. "I'm afraid you'll have to figure this one out on your own." The hologram started to disappear.

"Father?" Krypto called out. "Father!"

Strange lightning flashed in the sky. Krypto's eyes widened. "Aha! That must be the vile rodent, making more mischief!" He called out, "Don't worry, Superman! I WON'T REST UNTIL I FIND YOU!"

In the park where Superman and Krypto had played fetch, Ace, PB, Chip, and Merton lay on their backs staring up at the dark sky. It had been a long time since any of them had seen the stars.

"You know," Ace said peacefully, "I could rest here for the rest of my life."

Chip shot a bolt of lightning out of his claws and into the sky. Then he accidentally zapped Ace. "Oops," he said apologetically.

PB sighed contentedly. "I never knew the stars could be this beautiful." And there's so many of them. Look, there's one. There's another one. Look, there's one, too."

But Merton wasn't impressed. "These stars are crap!" she complained. "Wait till we get to the farm!"

Chip smiled a broad smile, showing his big front teeth. "Yeah, everything's better at the farm," he agreed dreamily.

Looking concerned, Ace turned to them and said, "Oh. Oh, yeah, about the farm. I wasn't exactly telling the—"

FLUMP.

A shadowy figure lumbered up to them and collapsed on the ground.

The shadowy figure was Krypto, not at his best. The fall, his time in the garbage pile, and the run to the park had left him looking the worse for wear. Exhausted and breathing heavily, he tried to ask where Lulu was. He thought Chip's flashes of lightning in the sky had come from the evil guinea pig. "Where is she?" Krypto gasped. "I'm sorry. I've never really run before. I usually pup up and away." He held one paw up, asking for a moment while he tried to catch his breath.

The four animals from the rescue shelter stared at him, concerned. "Are you okay?" PB asked.

"I'm fine, I'm fine," Krypto managed to say.

"Wait a minute," Ace said, trying to place Krypto. "Where do I know you from? I can't put my paw on it."

But Krypto just wanted an answer to his question. "WHERE IS SHE?" he repeated impatiently. Chip, startled by Krypto's sudden outburst, accidentally fired off another bolt of lightning. It hit the globe on top of a lamppost, shattering it.

Surprised, Krypto said, "Oh, so the powers I saw were YOURS!" He scowled. "You're working for the guinea pig!" he snarled.

"Lulu?" Ace scoffed. "We're not working for her."

"It's more of a she-left-us-to-die-in-a-fire type situation," Merton clarified.

"Getting super was a"—PB suddenly shrank to a tiny size, and her voice got small and high—"happy accident."

Krypto started to understand. "You can help me," he said slowly, then his voice quickened. "Hurry, there isn't much time. We have to save Superman!"

PB grew back to her normal size. Her eyes widened as she realized who they were talking to. "Oh my gosh! You're Krypto the Super-Dog!"

Ace nodded, finally remembering who the white dog was. "Of course. You're the freak who got me thrown back in the slammer. And froze my feet!"

"Oh, yes!" Krypto said. "You're the punk from the other day!"

Ace snarled, baring his teeth. He didn't like being called a punk.

"Look, man," Krypto pleaded. "I am desperate here. I lost my powers. And you all have powers." Despite his recent injuries, he managed to struggle onto a park bench. "And when one has an abundance of power," he explained seriously, "he or she has a certain duty to use that power to—"

SSSSS! Krypto's heartfelt speech was interrupted by the sound of Ace doing his business on a nearby statue. With his leg lifted, he said, "Sorry. You were saying something?"

"I was making an inspiring hero speech," Krypto said.

But Ace just kept going on . . . and on . . . and on . . .

"How much did you have to drink?" Krypto asked, amazed by how long this was taking.

Ace shrugged. "Two toilet bowls."

"Disgusting," Krypto said, grimacing.

Finally, Ace finished. "Pack, let's roll out." The four animals with superpowers started to walk past Krypto, leaving him behind.

"No!" Krypto cried desperately. "My best friend is in danger! You have to help me!"

But Ace just kept leading them away. "Sorry," he said. "We've got other plans."

"That's right!" Chip said enthusiastically. "We're going to the farm!"

Ace looked a little uncomfortable.

"Oh, yeah!" Merton agreed wholeheartedly. "Lettuce trees, baby!"

"Lettuce trees?" Krypto repeated suspiciously. "What's this farm called?"

"The Farm Upstate!" PB answered.

Krypto made a doubtful face. "That sounds made-up."

"How would you know?" Ace challenged, looking defiant.

"I grew up on a farm," Krypto answered. "Just outside a little town called Smallville."

It was Merton's turn to look doubtful. "Now, that sounds made-up."

Krypto was pretty sure Ace had invented this wonderful farm in his mind, but he didn't know why. "So, which way is this so-called farm?"

Ace's eyes darted. "Uh, it's upstate, so . . . up, obviously."

That settled it, as far as Krypto was concerned. Ace had to be lying. He turned to the three other animals and said, "Okay. He's not telling you the tru—"

"Can I see you for a sec?" Ace interrupted, pulling him aside. They walked a few feet away from the group, out of the others' earshot.

"You lied about the farm, didn't you?" Krypto asked accusingly.

"Big-time," Ace admitted. He cocked his head back toward the others. "Look, I had to give them some hope. No one was ever going to adopt us." He turned and looked at PB, Chip, and Merton. "So I promised them the farm would be their new home."

"You know, I'd be happy to take you and your friends to my farm," Krypto offered. "If you help me save Superman."

Ace thought about it for a moment. "Fine," he said, making up his mind. "We'll help you get your dumb owner back. You've got yourself a Super Team."

The two dogs shook paws on it.

But they had no idea what they were about to go up against.

12

In the classroom of a Metropolis elementary school, guinea pigs in cages contentedly chewed pale green leaves of lettuce. The students were gone for the day, and the teacher had given the guinea pigs lettuce just before she had left, too.

SMASH! Using the new powers granted to her by the sliver of Orange Kryptonite, Lulu crashed through the wall of the school and into the classroom. She addressed the guinea pigs, who kept right on chewing their lettuce.

"My fellow guinea pigs!" she proclaimed. "Brilliant, intelligent creatures! The world's most dominant species!"

The guinea pigs kept chewing. They had no idea who Lulu was, and as they ate their lettuce, they didn't look particularly brilliant or dominant.

Suddenly, Lulu felt a little shy. She wanted to share her magnificent plan with them, but to really get them on board, she needed to reveal what motivated her plan. And that was, well, a little personal. "Mm, how do I say this?" she said, hesitating. "Have you guys ever, like . . . liked someone?"

A guinea pig named Mark nodded toward the guinea pig next to him. "He likes the calico one."

Keith, the second guinea pig, was embarrassed to have his secret revealed right in front of his crush. "That was said in confidence," he said reproachfully.

"No," Lulu said, shaking her head. "I don't mean like, *like*-like, I mean more owner-and-pet like."

The guinea pigs looked confused. "Our owners are schoolchildren," the first guinea pig said.

"So many sticky hands," the second guinea pig said ruefully, looking a little shell-shocked from the experience of having kids pick him up repeatedly with their jelly-and-peanut-butter-covered fingers.

Lulu got a faraway look in her little eyes. "Mine was a diabolical genius," she said, thinking of her beloved Lex Luthor. "Not as smart as me, which is why this happened." Using her powers, she pulled a cart into the room with a TV on it, playing the news. Lois Lane gave the report.

"Thwarted by the Justice League, Lex Luthor now finds himself behind bars," Lois reported on the

TV. The screen showed Lex Luthor being hustled into a high-tech cell. CLANG! A guard slammed the door and its powerful electronic locks engaged automatically. Luthor grabbed the steel bars of the cell and shouted, "I'll destroy you all!"

Using a remote control, Lulu paused the broadcast on the shot of Lex Luthor. "That's my best friend and mentor."

The guinea pigs looked at each other. What was this all about?

Lulu hit Play to continue the news report. Lane said, "Built to house fearsome, superpowered criminals, Stryker's Island is the world's most inescapable prison." Lulu paused the report again.

"If I'm gonna get Lex outta that dump," Lulu explained, "I'm gonna need an army." She gestured with one of her front paws, and all the cages sprang open. Astonished, the guinea pigs stopped chewing. "But not just any army," she continued. "An unstoppable army."

She pulled the piece of Orange Kryptonite out from underneath the piece of Superman's cape that she'd tied around her neck. She held it up, and the guinea pigs were bathed in its orange glow.

CRASH! The Batmobile suddenly smashed

through the school wall, making another hole next to the gaping one Lulu had made when she'd crashed through. Batman leapt out of his sleek black race car.

"Not so fast!" he cried. "Lois Lane told us all about you, hamster."

"Hamster?" Lulu said, insulted by Batman's mistake. "A hamster is a hacky sack. A hamster is a mouse that had too much for lunch. We are guinea pigs. And when we're through with you, buster, you'll know it!"

Absorbing the cosmic energy from the Orange Kryptonite, the classroom guinea pigs POWERED UP! Mark found that he could shoot fire! Keith could blast ice! And Pigasus, sprouting wings, could soar through the air! They were ready for battle!

But they just stood there, waiting.

"What's going on?" Lulu demanded. "That was your cue to attack!"

"Oh, sorry," Mark apologized, gesturing toward Keith. "I was waiting for him to go first."

"Yeah," Keith said, "but if I went first, your fire would melt my ice, so maybe the wing lady should go first."

"I have a name," Pigasus objected.

Mark shook his head. "But if she goes first, I might

accidentally set her wings on fire, and I don't think any of us want that."

"Well, you don't want to get water on wings, either," Keith pointed out.

Mark looked confused. "Why?"

"It clogs the feathers," Keith explained.

"You're right," Mark agreed. "No, you're right. No, I'm sorry. So, do you wanna go first, or . . . ?"

"JUST GET THAT BATMAN!" Lulu shrieked, fed up with their babbling.

The superpowered guinea pigs finally shut up and attacked. They flew right into Batman. They shot fire at him. They shot ice at him. He fought back bravely, but he was outmatched. He was defeated by Lulu's guinea pig army.

"That was fun," Lulu said. "Now then, let's go free Lex—"

But as she tried to leave, she found she'd been snagged by Wonder Woman's magic lasso! "This ends now, sister," Wonder Woman warned her. "I have you in my Golden Lasso of Truth!"

"You want the truth?" Lulu said to Wonder Woman cattily. "Your boots are a bit much." The guinea pigs flew into action, battling with Wonder Woman. WHOOSH! ZWOOP! BAM!

In midtown Metropolis, Krypto and the shelter pets made their way down the sidewalk. PB was very excited. "You guys, check us out!" she squealed. "Like, look at us! We're just, like—we're a Super Team on a super mission and I figured out my super name! THE MIGHTY OINK!"

Chip grinned a toothy grin. "Can you believe it? Us, a Super Team!"

Krypto, leading the way, turned back and shot them a slightly exasperated look. "You're not a Super Team yet, okay? Sure, you have powers, but if you really wanna be heroes, you're gonna need the expertise of an expert. . . ." He realized he'd stepped in gum. Struggling to pull his paw free, he ripped out some of his fur. "YOWCH!"

"Sucks being mortal, huh?" Ace said, shooting him a look. "So, what happened to your powers, anyway?"

Krypto shrugged. "I ate some Green Kryptonite."

"A Kryptonian's only weakness!" PB said, priding herself on her knowledge of Super Heroes.

Merton looked baffled. "Why would you eat your weakness, ya dum-dum?" she asked disdainfully.

"It was in some cheese," Krypto admitted with a sheepish shrug.

"A dog's only weakness!" PB observed.

Ace thought about Krypto accidentally ingesting Green Kryptonite. "I ate a toy dinosaur once. If we're going off that, I'd say you've got a solid three days."

Krypto groaned.

13

PB did her best to cheer Krypto up. "At least you have us!" she enthused. Pointing to herself, she said, "Super Swine!" Pointing to Chip, she said, "The Furocious Zapper!" Pointing to Ace, she said, "Indestructidog! And . . . wait. Where's Snap-er-ella? Snaps?"

Merton had stopped to talk to a helmet with a headlamp. She was so nearsighted, she thought the helmet was a cute male turtle. "What's happening, sweet cheeks? Whaddya say? Your shell or mine?"

PB spotted a row of TVs in the window of an electronics store. When she saw what was playing on their screens, she stopped and pointed. "You guys, look!"

The five animals crowded around the window. On the screens, they saw Lulu flying through the air. She and the other guinea pigs were battling Wonder Woman!

"Mm-kay," PB said, full of admiration for her hero. "Wonder Woman will stop her!"

But the next shot on the TV screens showed Wonder

Woman tied up with her own magic lasso. "Goddess, no!" PB cried.

Next, the TVs showed The Flash with his feet stuck in blocks of cement. Aquaman rode a wave out of the sewers, only to have the water frozen, which sent him flying off and landing hard on the pavement. Cyborg tried to help his fellow Justice League Super Heroes, but Lulu yanked out his battery. He immediately slumped over.

Finally, Lulu used her tractor-beam power to steal Green Lantern's ring and capture her. The guinea pigs had won!

Ace, PB, Chip, and Merton looked horrified.

"I guess it's down to us," Krypto said. "Who's ready to go save my best friend?"

Chip stared at him with his big, round eyes. "You want us to fight her? She just took out the whole Justice League. We don't stand a chance!"

Merton said goodbye to the helmet with the headlamp as though she were going off to war, never to return. "Remember me when I'm gone, Fabrizio."

"Guys, relax," Krypto assured them. "We'll be fine."

But they didn't feel fine. Chip cowered behind his bushy tail. A piece of Merton's shell fell off.

They made their way to a rooftop for a better view of Lulu and her guinea pig army. Looking down, they saw the guinea pigs terrorizing the city—smashing, freezing, and burning buildings and cars at will.

"You see?" Krypto said confidently. "Totally fine. Now, let's hero up! All right, team, what are your stats?"

PB stepped forward, excited. "Okay, my name's PB. I'm a Pisces. I love the smell of fresh linen and other things that smell fresh."

"Just tell me your powers," Krypto said. "Like, for example, my powers include heat vision, freeze breath, and the Solar Paw Punch."

Ace looked unimpressed. "So basically you see hot, you breathe cold, and you punch stuff?"

"I'll have you know," Krypto said, drawing himself up and looking slightly offended at Ace's question, "the Solar Paw Punch is so intense, I've never even attempted it. It requires me to fly all the way to your yellow sun and absorb its deadly radiation directly into my cells. Which could kill me!"

Ace rolled his eyes. "Like I said, you punch stuff."

Just then, the five animals heard chaotic noises. Hurrying to the edge of the roof, they looked down at the square in front of the city's newspaper, the *Daily Planet*. In the middle of the square was a big globe with DAILY PLANET printed on it.

Lulu and her guinea pigs were still using their superpowers to wreak havoc on the citizens of Metropolis. Satisfied with the damage they'd done, Lulu told her minions, "Okay, enough mayhem. Thank you. We gotta go." But then she looked up and spotted her old shelter mates. She was surprised, since she'd assumed they'd perished in the fire. "Ooh, my goodness!" she exclaimed. "Look who's alive! Well, let's correct that little oversight, shall we?" She gestured for her army to attack!

"Ace," Krypto quickly commanded, "deploy canine shield!"

Ace looked confused. "What is a canine—"

Knowing Ace was invulnerable, Krypto shoved him in front as they jumped down to fight the guinea pigs. Mark breathed fire at them. "Evade!" Krypto cried. He, Chip, Merton, and PB jumped away as the flames engulfed Ace.

Scorched and smoldering but unhurt, Ace asked, "Anybody wanna switch powers?"

Krypto and PB charged at the guinea pigs. "You're up, pig!" Krypto shouted.

PB shut her eyes tight, trying to summon her ability to grow. "Okay, PB," she said to herself, "think BIG!"

BLOOP! Instead of growing, PB shrank! She found herself running among gigantic guinea pig paws and enormous human feet, dodging to avoid being squished. "AAAAHHHHHH!" she screamed in her tiny, squeaky voice.

Krypto called on his next Super-Pet. "Squirrel, light 'em up!"

Chip concentrated, forming a ball of lightning in his paw. He prepared to blast the rapidly approaching guinea pigs, but when he looked into their eyes, he froze. "No, no, I can't!"

"Of course you can!" Krypto urged. "I mean, what's the worst that could happen?"

The squirrel looked down at the electricity bubbling out of his paws and said, "I could hurt someone. Or they could hurt me! Or maybe me freezing like this is the worst thing—"

ZZZZZT! Keith blasted Chip with his freeze ray, immobilizing him like a frosty squirrel statue!

Krypto turned to Merton. "Turtle, use your speed and get them!"

"On it!" Merton shouted. She took off in a flash, zipping back and forth and finally coming to a screeching stop in the middle of nowhere. She looked around. "Where the heck am I?"

Krypto was frustrated. "You guys are really terrible Super Heroes. I don't understand why you're not getting this!"

"There's a lot you don't understand about us," Ace countered. "Maybe if you'd just pay attention."

"Oh, I'm paying attention," Krypto claimed. "One hundo percent attention." But right at that moment, Krypto failed to notice that behind him, a guinea pig named Nutmeg had grabbed Ace in a full nelson wrestling hold. "Help . . . ," Ace gurgled.

But Krypto had spotted Lulu. Growling, he ran through the battle, dodging combatants, making his way toward the evil guinea pig. He pounced, but Lulu used her Orange Kryptonite powers to stop him in midair.

"Risky move for a dog with no powers," she said calmly. "Some would say heroic. I would say dumb."

"Where is Superman?" Krypto demanded.

Lulu shook her head, clucking her tongue sympathetically. "I'm not telling. Classic evil! Lex would be so proud."

Krypto couldn't believe what he was hearing. "This is really about Lex Luthor? Don't you understand? He was testing on you—"

"We were colleagues," Lulu corrected. "We were scientists together."

"You were the guinea pig," Krypto insisted. "Your hair fell out."

For a moment, Lulu was stumped. The dog had a point. Her hair had fallen out. But then she thought of something. "Yeah, just like his did! Lex needed me. That's more than I can say for your Superman."

"Superman needed me," Krypto said. Then he caught himself using the past tense. "He needs me."

Lulu started to circle the helpless dog, who was frozen in place. She was enjoying filling his head with doubts. "Does he?" she asked. "And why do you think he was in the shelter that day?"

Krypto really didn't have a good answer for that one. "He was . . . he was . . ."

"He was getting you a friend so that you'd give him some space," Lulu said, answering her own question. Using her powers, she lifted Krypto's floppy ear and whispered into it. "Him and his fiancée."

Krypto looked absolutely stunned. He had no idea that Superman wanted to marry Lois!

"Oh, no," Lulu said, pretending to be shocked. "You didn't know. I really am sorry, because this must be so painful to have to hear from me." She dropped her fake voice of concern. "Face it, buster. Superman's moved on. But don't worry—I'm sure you can crash at the Hall of Justice." She then used her powers to hurl Krypto all the way to the Hall of Justice and drop him on the front steps. WHUMP!

"Wow, she threw that dog real far," Merton said.

"Uh, he's probably fine," Ace said, not really believing his own words, but wanting to reassure the others. "I mean, he's got a hard head."

Lulu faced the Super-Pets, grinning. "You know what's funny?" she said. "For a minute I was worried when I saw that the Orange Kryptonite gave you powers." She snorted with laughter. "But then I remembered—you're *you*."

The Super-Pets hung their heads, humiliated by their defeat at the paws of Lulu's guinea pig army. Lulu sauntered off, calmly calling to her minions, "Come on! Let's go, little piggies!" She floated away, followed by her furry soldiers.

Later that day, Lois Lane interviewed Lex Luthor in his cell. He and his assistant, Mercy, were being held in separate high-tech cells on Stryker's Island, a maximum-security prison guarded by powerful robots.

"Don't play coy, Luthor," Lois told the prisoner. "I know you're behind this." She held up a notepad computer. On its screen, Lulu and her guinea pigs were causing mayhem in Daily Square.

Lex Luthor gave her a cold smile. "Impressive destruction, but not my work."

"Oh, really?" Lois asked. She paused the video and zoomed in on Lulu's ear. Lois saw that the laboratory tag attached to it read LEXCORP.

"Huh," Lex Luthor said smugly. "Looks like one of my little babies is all grown up."

"Someday I'd love to work for someone who's not

Lex Luthor," Mercy said from her cell next to the bald Super-Villain's.

"Spill it, Lex," Lois said in a tough voice. "What have you done with Superman?"

The bald Super-Villain Luthor shrugged. "Wherever Superman is, it's got nothing to do with me or my company, LexCorp International."

But at that very moment, in LexCorp's soaring glass tower, Mark and Keith were using their combined powers to construct a large aquarium tank—where Aquaman was imprisoned.

Nearby, The Flash was trapped in a giant hamster wheel, running nonstop. Batman, Wonder Woman, Cyborg, and Green Lantern were locked in human-sized cage-like cells.

And Superman struggled to escape from a Green Kryptonite sphere.

But it was no use. All the members of the Justice League were ensnared in LexCorp Tower, held there by Lulu and her powerful assistants.

As Mark and Keith put the finishing touches on Aquaman's holding tank, he told them, "You think that you've trapped Aquaman, but you've made one giant mistake, because I—" Just then, flakes of fish food floated down from above, distracting the aquatic Super Hero.

"Fish food!" he exclaimed happily. "Yum-yum-yum-yum-yum."

15

The guinea pigs turned on a television and settled down to watch. Mark played footage of Keith getting run over by Krypto as he barreled toward Lulu, intent on stopping her.

"Hey, have you seen this?" Mark said, relishing the embarrassing video.

"Oh, no," Keith protested. "I don't think anyone wants to see that."

"The wing lady definitely wants to see it," Mark teased.

"I have a name," Pigasus said.

Mark showed the footage of Keith getting bowled over by Krypto. "Thank you," Keith said sarcastically, "for making me relive that in front of my peers."

"See your face?" Mark said, pointing at the screen. "It's a mix of horror but also knowing that this is as good as it's going to get."

While the guinea pigs talked in front of the TV, the Super Heroes of the Justice League heard only little guinea pig squeaks and grunts with their human ears.

"Aww, come on!" Batman complained. "I can't believe we got beaten by a bunch of muskrats."

"Vic, can you translate what they're saying?" Wonder Woman asked.

Cyborg shook his half-human, half-robotic head. "I can't do anything while they've got me stuck in airplane mode."

The TV was playing live news coverage of Lois Lane reporting from the prison on Stryker's Island. "While this reporter continues her search for the truth," Lois said, "it seems Superman's dog is also on the case." A video clip showed Krypto and his four fellow Super-Pets facing off against Lulu's guinea pigs in Daily Square.

"Krypto?" Superman said, his eyes widening at the sight of his friend on the TV.

"Of course!" Cyborg enthused. "He'll save us!"

But then the news report showed Lulu dropping Krypto on the steps of the Hall of Justice. He lay there unconscious.

"No!" Superman cried, concerned for his best friend. "He doesn't have his powers!"

On the TV, Lulu's guinea pigs sent the huge *Daily*

Planet globe rolling off its stand and hurtling toward the innocent citizens of Metropolis. Ace, impervious to pain, stopped the gigantic globe before it hurt anyone.

"But those other pets do," Wonder Woman observed.

"So can't Krypto work with them to save the city?" Green Lantern asked.

Superman looked uncomfortable. "Yeah, about that," he said, hesitating. "He's not the greatest with other animals."

"Well, he'd better get it together soon," Batman warned, "or those ferrets are gonna take over the world!" He looked at the guinea pigs and shivered in horror.

Outside the magnificent entrance to the Hall of Justice, Krypto lay still on the marble. Ace, PB, Chip, and Merton sat around him, watching for signs of life.

"Is he okay?" Chip asked, worried.

"Looks like he's still breathing," PB said.

Chip leaned in for a closer look. "Yep, he's alive."

Merton turned to Ace with a triumphant look in her cloudy eyes. "Pay up, dog." Ace handed her a piece of lettuce.

Coming to, Krypto opened one blurry eye in time to see this exchange. "You bet on whether I was alive?" he groaned.

"Nope," Ace said. "I bet on whether you were dead."

"I bet that you would be the first one of us to have a baby," Chip admitted.

"What a fun game," Krypto said bitterly.

Ace looked up at the polished stone columns and arches of the Hall of Justice. "So, what is this place, anyway? Some kind of fancy Department of Motor Vehicles?"

PB couldn't believe he was asking that. "Are you kidding? This is the Hall of Justice!"

The pets all gazed up at the impressive building.

"This is where the Justice League hangs out," PB continued. "I bet they're all super best friends and they tell each other everything."

Krypto looked up at the stained glass window showing Superman in a heroic pose and thought about his friend's secret engagement to Lois. "Yeah, everything," he said in a small, unhappy voice.

He got to his feet and walked into the Hall of Justice through a doggy door. PB and the other Super-Pets looked worried.

"He seems sad and defeated," Merton said.

"So it is a Department of Motor Vehicles!" Ace said.

"Maybe one of us should go talk to him," Chip suggested.

"Not it," Ace said quickly.

"Come on, Ace," PB pleaded. "You always know what to say."

The others looked at Ace hopefully. He sighed and reluctantly trotted through the doggy door after Krypto.

Ace found Krypto up on the building's rooftop, staring at a beautiful sunset. Ace started to cross the roof toward Krypto, but the Super-Dog warned, "Watch out for the—"

BUMP! Ace walked right into something.

"Invisible Jet," Krypto finished. He knew from painful experience exactly where Wonder Woman always parked her amazing transparent jet plane. "I just want to be alone," he told Ace.

But Ace ignored Krypto's request, walking up over

to him. Rubbing his bumped nose, he said, "This is the best place to watch the sunset. If you want to be alone, why don't you go someplace uglier? Besides, don't you want to save your Superman?"

"Of course I do," Krypto said quietly. "He's my best friend. At least, I thought he was. Things are changing so fast, he didn't even tell me he was getting married."

"That's what's got your leash all twisted, huh?" Ace said, sitting down next to him. "Yeah, well," he sighed, "people are complicated."

Krypto raised an eyebrow. What did Ace know about people? Wasn't he a stray who'd always lived on the streets? "How would you know?" he asked.

Ace stared out at the horizon in the distance, looking a bit wistful. Krypto noticed his mood, wondering what had made him sad.

"Aw," Ace said, "forget it."

Suddenly, Krypto realized something. He turned to Ace and said, "You had an owner."

16

Ace kept his gaze forward, trying to look as though nothing ever bothered him. Krypto could tell he really didn't want to talk about it.

"Right, that's your business," he said. "I am not going to pry." But a moment later, he asked, "Was he nice?"

After a long pause, Ace said quietly, "They. My owner was a family. A mom. A dad. And her."

Ace remembered exactly what had happened years before, and described everything to Krypto. . . .

A man, a woman, and their toddler daughter had brought Ace into their home when he was just a puppy. The dad filled a bowl with dry dog food, and Ace dove his entire body into the bowl, delighted.

In the kitchen sink, the mom gave Ace and the little girl a bath together.

In the toddler's room, Ace lay on the carpeted floor. The little girl rubbed his tummy with her bare feet.

One day, the mom and dad were rushing around

their upstairs bedroom getting dressed for an event. Ace lay on their bed. Distracted, the parents didn't notice their little girl toddling out of the bedroom and toward the staircase. She tottered in front of the stairs. Ace jumped off the bed and ran to her. Just as she was about to step off and fall down the stairs, Ace grabbed hold of her wrist in his jaws and pulled her back to safety.

The parents heard their daughter crying. They ran over to find her in tears. A tiny trickle of blood was running down her wrist from Ace's bite.

The next thing he knew, Ace found himself at the animal rescue shelter, locked in a cage, never to see his owners again.

Ace sat on the roof, staring out at the city's sky-scrapers and the clouds moving through the sky above them.

"Ace," Krypto said, "what you did for that little girl . . ."

"Eh, it was nothing," Ace shrugged. "I just did what any dog would do."

"And then they just"—Krypto could barely bring himself to say the awful words—"gave you away?"

"I don't blame 'em," Ace said in a small, hurt voice. "They thought were protecting their kid."

"But you saved her," Krypto said.

"And I'd do it again," Ace said. "Worst day of my life, but I wouldn't change a thing about it."

"Why not?" Krypto asked.

Ace turned and looked right at Krypto. "When you love somebody, and I mean you really love them, you have to be willing to do anything for them. Even if that means letting them go."

"Even if it hurts?" Krypto asked.

"Especially then," Ace told him. "You know what they say about dogs, don't you?"

"Never feed us chocolate?"

"We love unconditionally," Ace said.

Krypto took it in, nodding slowly, realizing the truth of this. Then he thought of something. "Maybe it's not too late for you. To find another family."

Shaking his head, Ace said, "No, that ship sailed a long time ago. But it's all right. Because I got another boat." He looked over the edge of the roof and down at PB, Chip, and Merton. They were practicing using their new powers, trying to gain control over them.

Zipping around, Merton bumped into a statue. "Excuse me, sir," she said politely, mistaking the statue for a live human being.

Krypto watched them, too. It wasn't impressive. "I think your boat has sprung a leak," he said candidly.

"Those guys?" Ace said. "Well, they suck visibly,

yes. I can agree with you there. But they're stronger than you think."

PB tried to control her amazing ability to change sizes. But she just shrank and grew, seemingly at random. Big, little, big, little, big, little . . .

"PB just needs a little love," Ace said.

Chip practiced forming lightning with his paws. But he only succeeded in accidentally zapping the ground and lifting into the air—scaring himself.

"Chip needs to feel safe," Ace said.

Merton wasn't trying out her incredible speed. Instead, she appeared to be deep in conversation with the statue.

"And Merton," Ace said, "needs leafy greens."

Krypto nodded, admiring Ace's insights. "You really know them, huh?"

"It's called listening," Ace said, shrugging. "You learn a lot about someone when you're locked up with them forever."

Getting an idea, Krypto said, "Wait a minute. Lulu was in the shelter with you, too. What'd you learn about her?"

Ace snorted. "All that guinea pig ever talked about was world domination and some bald dude with nice hands."

"Lex!" Krypto gasped. "Of course!" In the distance,

he could see Stryker's Island. "Stryker's Island," he continued. "Lulu must be going there to spring him!"

"Then that's where we'll go!" Ace said, getting up. "Come on!" He started running toward the stairs that led down from the roof.

Krypto called after him, "Watch out for the—"

BUMP!

Ace smacked right into Wonder Woman's Invisible Jet again. "OOF!" he grunted. "Invisible Jet, yup."

Krypto was absolutely right about Lulu's plan. She and her guinea pig army headed straight to Stryker's Island to free her beloved mentor, Lex Luthor, from his imprisonment. The mayhem they'd caused around Daily Square had just been a warm-up—a chance for all the guinea pigs to get used to fighting with their new powers granted by the Orange Kryptonite. Now it was time to put their combat skills to the test against the robot guards of Stryker's Island.

They passed the test.

The robots, designed and programmed to defend the maximum-security fortress against human invaders, didn't stand a chance against an army of guinea pigs with awesome powers granted by the remains of an alien planet. Using their powers of fire, ice, flight, strength, and more, Lulu's rodents wiped out the robots in no time flat.

In a smoky, nondescript room inside the prison, a legion of robots lay damaged and defeated. One robot

KRYPTO

Krypto is a Super-Dog with amazing powers—just like his lifelong best friend, **Superman**—including flight, freeze breath, heat vision, and super-hearing.

ACE

Ace and Batman team up to be a Dynamic Duo! Ace has super-strength and indestructability, which make him a perfect partner for the Dark Knight as he fights crime.

Move over, injustice—**PB** has the ability to change her size from **ENORMOUS** to SUPER SMALL, and she's going to use that power to help her hero, **Wonder Woman**, save the day!

MERTON

The Flash meets his match—and new best friend—in **Merton**, a turtle with super-speed. Together, these two run circles around the bad guys.

CHIP

Sparks fly when **Chip** the squirrel uses his power to throw electrical bolts to help **Green Lantern** dispel the darkness and bring light to those in need.

Energized by Orange Kryptonite, **Lulu** the guinea pig sets out to destroy the Justice League and take over Metropolis with her terrible mind powers.

LULU EVIL GENIUS

Lulu uses the Orange Kryptonite to create a team of powerful guinea pigs, each with their own unique ability. These guinea pigs may have superpowers, but they are no match for . . .

. . . **THE DC LEAGUE OF SUPER PETS** and **THE JUSTICE LEAGUE**.

Krypto, Ace, and the other pets join forces to stop Lulu and save Metropolis!

POW!

was still sounding the alarm, calling out, "Intruder! Intruder! Intruder!" The guinea pig named Nutmeg, who had nearly strangled Ace at Daily Square, ripped the robot's head off. Wires stuck out of his metal neck.

Mark blasted flame at another robot. Proud of his success, Mark high-fived Pigasus, accidentally setting her on fire. Keith extinguished the blaze and shook his head.

Lulu addressed her guinea pig army. "This is it," she said triumphantly. "I'm going to see Lex again. Finally, the two great minds of our generation back together. Luthor and Lulu! Or Lulu and Luthor! Lu-Luthor! How's my hair? I don't want to freak him out."

Mark and Keith looked at each other. What were they supposed to say? Lulu was bald!

"Bald is beautiful!" Keith exclaimed.

"Stunning!" Mark offered.

Lulu shook it off. "You know what? I'm overthinking it. Your pet's coming for you, Lexie!"

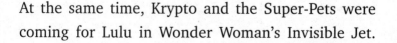

At the same time, Krypto and the Super-Pets were coming for Lulu in Wonder Woman's Invisible Jet.

Krypto was in the pilot's seat, with Ace, PB, Chip, and Merton crammed into the cockpit with him.

"Oh my gosh," PB gasped, absolutely thrilled. "Wonder Woman has sat right where I'm sitting! Actually, I feel like I am her, because I'm in her stance and in her seat. Do you think I smell like her now?"

"More important," Ace said, addressing Krypto, "do you know how to fly this thing?"

"Relax," Krypto scoffed. "We'll be fine!"

BOOM! Something hit the jet, sending it plummeting!

"Stop saying that!" Ace shouted at Krypto.

CRASH! The jet slammed into the ground, right at the foot of a bridge leading across the water to Stryker's Island. The Super-Pets emerged from the jet, shaken. "Who shot us down?" PB said. "Wonder Woman's Invisible Jet is invisible!"

"It's really more transparent," said a familiar voice as a figure emerged from a cloud of dust. It was . . . Whiskers, the adorable kitten from the animal shelter!

"Whiskers?" the Super Pets all said, amazed.

"Out of the way, cat child," Krypto commanded. "We have to get to Stryker's."

"Sorry, I can't do that," Whiskers said in her sweet

little voice. "Lulu saved my life. Now I must take yours. Goodbye!"

ZHWAM! ZHWIM! ZHWOOMP! ZHWOMP! Using the Orange Kryptonite powers Lulu had given her, Whiskers fired four orange, glowing whisker rockets out of her tail at the Super-Pets! They dove, rolled, and ran to escape from her attack.

BOOM! Another explosive whisker rocket landed, dividing the group in two. Krypto and PB were launched into the air, landing on the scaffolding of a construction site. Krypto looked to PB.

"PB," he said urgently, "I need you to grow big and—"

But when she tried to grow, PB accidentally shrank until she was so small, she fell through the gaps in the scaffolding.

"Or the complete opposite," Krypto said. "Totally fine." He quickly but carefully made his way down the scaffolding and rejoined PB.

Whiskers chased Ace, Chip, and Merton, firing orange blasts at them with her tail. "What do we do now?" Chip shouted.

"In here!" Ace answered, diving for cover in a parked car and setting off its alarm. Krypto and PB joined them, scurrying into the parked car without being seen by Whiskers. Once she was in the car, PB tried to grow back to her normal size, but she overshot the mark. Everyone was smashed up against the car windows.

Unfortunately, Whiskers heard the alarm and headed toward the row of parked cars, figuring her prey had to be hiding in one of them.

Up on the construction site, PB was entangled in a wire dangled from a crane. Krypto came down and tried to help her, but he ended up tangled, too. They slowly spun around, caught.

Referring to Whiskers, Krypto noted, "That creature may be little, but she packs a punch."

"I know. I just can't control it!" said PB. Then she confided, "Even with powers . . . I'm nothing like Wonder Woman."

"PB, there's something you should know about Wonder Woman," Krypto replied.

"Praise be her name," PB sighed, casting her gaze up to heaven.

"Diana is fiercely independent," Krypto continued, getting PB's attention back. "Completely her own woman. And if you really wanna be like her, you'll be yourself."

PB beamed. Encouraged by Krypto, she shrank

back down to her normal size, freeing the others to move inside the car.

As she approached the line of parked cars, stalking her prey, Whiskers laughed a cute but frightening laugh.

"Okay, Chip," Krypto ordered. "Time to light that kitty up!"

Chip looked panicked. "Me? Light her up? With the terrifying lightning powers I wish I didn't have? Is that what you're asking?"

Krypto saw the charge building up in Chip's paw. "You've got to take a risk, buddy. Because you know what's really scary?"

"That demonic laser cat?" Chip guessed.

"Living your whole life scared," Krypto told the nervous squirrel.

Shivering, Chip said, "That is scary." He nodded, growing more confident. "Okay, you can do this, Chip," he told himself. "Take a risk!"

CRACKLE! Chip fired his dazzling bolt of electricity up through the open moonroof. CRASH! The lightning hit the balcony of a building, knocking off a potted plant. It fell through the moonroof and broke into pieces . . . on Krypto's head. The dog was knocked out cold.

Seeing that Krypto had used knowledge of Chip's personality to motivate him, Merton walked over to Krypto, unaware that he was unconscious. She began to share the tale of her long life with him. "All right, you dragged my backstory out of me. It all started in Central City in eighteen fifty-four . . ."

ZWHAM! BOOM! Whiskers blew up car after car, making her way down the line of parked vehicles toward the one the Super-Pets were hiding in. "I'm just a sweet little *purr-purr* baby!" she called. "Why won't you play with me?"

Inside the car, Merton was still sharing her life story. "And I had a whole period in the sixties when I was basically a full-time alchemist . . ."

Krypto came to and shook his head. "Merton," he said, "we don't have time." Searching through the car, he found a pair of purple glasses and handed them to the nearsighted turtle. "Here. Try these!"

Merton took the purple glasses and put them on. Instantly, she could see much more clearly! "Whoa!" she said, staring through the glasses at the other Super-Pets. "None of you are turtles? This explains so much."

"Super-Pets!" Whiskers called. "Come out and play!"

"That monster is lucky I don't have my heat vision," Krypto said.

"Good thing you've got something better," PB said proudly.

Krypto looked confused. "What's that?"

"Us!" Merton told him.

Ace smiled. Krypto had done it. He'd given the others the confidence they needed to wield their new powers effectively.

Krypto looked touched, happy to be accepted by the gang. "Okay, pack," he said. "I have a plan." He smiled.

As Whisker worked her way along the parked cars, Whiskers noticed a rattling noise from one up ahead. She grinned. The Super-Pets must be inside! She coughed up a hairball grenade and threw it at the car. "Goodbye!" she called in her sweet little voice.

BOOM! The car was launched into the air! It flipped over and landed on its side. As the smoke cleared, Whiskers padded up to it on her soft paws to look inside for her victims. But the car was empty!

"What's the matter?" Krypto asked from behind her. "Cat got your tongue?"

Whiskers whipped around and saw Krypto standing alone. She fired a whisker rocket at him. FWOOM!

"NOW!" Krypto yelled. Ace leapt out and put himself between Whiskers and Krypto, absorbing the impact of the rocket with his invulnerable body!

Whisker threw another grenade, but Merton zipped forward, caught the explosive, zoomed all around the city (pausing only to "borrow" some lettuce from a guy making a salad), and returned to place the grenade next to Whiskers.

At the same time, PB expanded to an enormous

size and kicked a dumpster with her back legs, launching it into the sky.

With the grenade next to Whiskers, and the shadow of the falling dumpster growing around them, Merton said, "Meow-meow buh-bye!" and then sped away.

"Uh-oh . . . ," Whiskers said.

WHAM! The dumpster landed upside down right over Whiskers. Chip charged up his paws and fired electricity at the base of the dumpster, melting its metal rim so it stuck to the ground.

KABOOM! The grenade exploded inside the sealed dumpster.

Chip winced at the sound of the explosion. "What did we just do to that kitten?" he asked, wide-eyed.

Whiskers cried out from inside the dumpster, her voice echoing around the metal chamber, "I still have eight more lives!"

"Nice job, team!" Krypto said, congratulating them. But their work was far from done. "Come on!" he shouted as he ran toward the bridge leading over the water to Stryker's Island. The four other Super-Pets raced after him.

From their cells in LexCorp Tower, the Super Heroes of the Justice League watched a news report on TV. Onscreen, Lois Lane reported, "The threat was neutered, thanks to Krypto and friends. Pretty sure that was a hairball grenade, so this is our world now." Helicopter footage showed Krypto and his friends running past smoldering buildings.

Superman lit up with pride. "This is amazing!"

"Yes, humanity is saved!" Wonder Woman said.

"No, my baby's made friends!" Superman said.

Wonder Woman, Batman, Aquaman, Green Lantern, and The Flash just stared at Superman like he'd lost his mind. His baby?

Noticing them staring at him, Superman explained, "If you all had pets, you'd understand."

The Super Heroes thought about this.

"You know," The Flash mused, remembering, "I had a cheetah once, but she ate my landlord. And tore up my couch. Man, I loved that couch."

"On the planet Oa," Green Lantern said, "I thought I had a pet raccoon. But he thought we were dating."

Aquaman swam up to the edge of his tank to share his comment on the topic of pet ownership. "All the creatures of the sea are my friends. Except for one eel, who knows what he did."

"I'm not really an animal guy," Batman admitted.

"Huh," Superman said. "Are you allergic, or what?"

"As a child I fell into a well filled with bats," Batman explained. "I can still hear my screams as their dark wings flapped around me, scratching my chubby, child flesh. I'm still tormented by that terrifying memory every waking moment of my life."

Superman stared at him. "I really think a pet would be good for you."

19

On Stryker's Island, explosions rumbled through the prison as Lulu's guinea pigs battled the human guards inside the fortress. Lex sat in his prison cell, wondering what was going on. Was someone coming to free him?

CRASH! Lulu broke through the ceiling from the floor above and flew down into the large chamber next to Lex's cell. Guinea pigs quickly overcame the guards, then left their leader alone with her mentor.

"Lex!" she cried joyfully. "I'm here! We're finally reunited!"

All Luthor and Mercy heard were little high-pitched squeaks and grunts. But the Super-Villain recognized his lab-test subject from Lois Lane's interview. "Ahh," he said. "The student returns to the teacher."

"Oh, good," Mercy said sarcastically from her cell. "Your marmot baby."

"Shut it," Lulu snapped at Mercy. "I'm his favorite henchman, not you."

Again, this just sounded like a series of squeaks to

Mercy and Luthor. The humans shared a look, unsure of what the guinea pig was trying to tell them.

Lulu floated herself and a smartphone up to Luthor's face. "Now, I have a present for you. It's not here, but I have pictures of it on my phone." She swiped through pictures of the Justice League Super Heroes trapped in individualized cells, narrating as she went. "Loser. Loser. Look at their dumb outfits."

Lex Luthor was pleased and impressed. "My evil plan to take out the Justice League." Chuckling, he said, "Wow. You really did study."

"Oh, and wait until you see this," Lulu said, intending to show him more pictures of the imprisoned Super Heroes. Swiping, she landed on a picture of a human owner petting a cat, except she'd Photoshopped her own face onto the cat's body and Luthor's face onto the human's. Embarrassed, she said, "Okay, I don't know how that got in there. No one wants that, right? Well, clearly I've been hacked." She decided to change the subject. Putting her phone away, Lulu said, "Let's get you out of here."

Just outside the locked cell, the robot guard lay slumped on the floor, unconscious. Lulu used her powers to lift its face toward a scanner. Once the scanner could read its eyes, it would unlock the door to the cell.

"Oh, I can't believe this is finally happening," Lulu squeaked, thrilled to be freeing Lex Luthor.

Without understanding Lulu's squeaks, Mercy watched the guinea pig use her mind to lift the robot's face and said, "I can't believe this is actually happening."

But just as the unconscious guard's eyes were about to reach the scanner . . . WHAM! PB crashed through the hole in the ceiling, landing right on Lulu! She rolled off the guinea pig, and Chip zapped Lulu with a bolt of electricity. ZZZAP!

"This ends now, rodent!" Krypto announced.

"You were just defeated by the League of Super-Pets!" PB cheered, celebrating.

Merton pretended a phone was ringing. "Brring-brring! Hello! Who's there? The League of Super-Pets!"

"Give it up, Lulu!" Ace barked. "It's over."

As the team of Super-Pets prepared to bring Lulu to justice, she pretended to be afraid. "Oh, no! You're actually getting the hang of using superpowers as a team! I'm toast! I'm a goner! NOT!" Using her own power, she pulled a heavy metal filing cabinet from the room above, making it hover right over Krypto.

"No!" Ace cried.

"One more step and the puppy gets it," Lulu

warned. "Unless your friends walk into those cells over there." She nodded toward a row of empty high-tech cells lining the wall.

"Ace, attack!" Krypto shouted. "I'll be fine!"

"You'll be a pancake," Lulu said.

Panic played across the faces of Ace, Chip, PB, and Merton. What could they possibly do? If they used their powers to attack Lulu, she'd drop the heavy filing cabinet on Krypto. He didn't have his powers to protect him. It'd be the end of him!

"Okay," Lulu said. "I'm gonna count to three. And I'll start at two 'cause I'm evil. Two—"

"All right, Lulu," Ace said, seeing no alternative. "You win."

"No!" Krypto cried. "Don't listen to her!"

"What choice do I have?" Ace said, turning to him.

"Oh, I didn't know they were going to be so sad," Lulu said sarcastically. "Aww, he doesn't want to go in the cell. But he has to, to save the other one." As the four Super-Pets walked into their cells, Lulu said, "Everyone is upset." She threw Krypto into his own cell and slammed the door shut. It automatically locked, engaging its high-tech, unbreakable bars and bolts to make escape impossible.

Now that Krypto was out from under the filing cabinet, the Super-Pets tried to use their own powers to escape from the cells, but their efforts failed. "You fools!" Lulu taunted. "You can't get out of those cells! "You're not powerful enough!"

Turning away from the holding cells, Lulu got back to business.

"Okay—now, then. Where was I?" She lifted the robot guard off the floor and placed its face against the scanner so it could read its eyes. Flashing green, the scanner unlocked the door to Luthor's cell. CLANG! The door swung open. Lex Luthor was free.

He stepped out and offered Lulu his hand. "Let me look at you, my pet."

"Oh, Lex!" Lulu gushed, thrilled.

His hands joined to her paws and they spun slowly around. Lulu was in heaven. Luthor patted her on the head—then swung her into the cell he'd just left and slammed the door shut!

"Lex!" Lulu cried, baffled by what had just happened. "Lex, what are you doing? We're a team. Lex, we were scientists together! No! Lex, what are you doing?"

Ignoring the guinea pig's squeaks and grunts, Luthor picked up the robot guard and used its eyes to unlock the door to Mercy's cell. She stepped out into the large room.

"I mean, come on," Luthor said. "You didn't expect me to share credit with a rodent, did you?"

As they left together, Mercy turned back and gave Lulu a smug look. Watching them go, Lulu's heart was breaking. Though she tried to use all her power, she couldn't break out of the maximum-security cell. "LEX!" she sobbed.

"Oh, what a surprising little turn of events," Merton said with satisfaction.

20

Her spirit crushed by Luthor's betrayal, Lulu fell back in her cell.

But Krypto wasn't giving up hope. He saw an opportunity to turn Lulu against Lex Luthor. Maybe he could even get her to help them save Superman. "Lulu," he said. "Join our pack. If we work together, we can get out of here and save Superman. He's still alive."

"For fifty-six minutes, he is," Lulu clarified. She held up her phone, showing a live feed of a ticking clock. "When this clock hits zero, the entire Justice League is gonna go kaboom! You're about to have a front-row seat for the end of Superman."

"No!" Krypto cried.

Smiling a cold, thin smile, Lulu shrugged. "If I can't have my guy, you can't have yours."

"Only one problem, genius," Merton pointed out. "You aren't powerful enough to get outta that cell."

But just as Merton said this, Mark and Keith arrived.

Lulu lit up when she saw them. "Mark! Keith! Get me out of this cell! NOW!"

"Okay," Mark said.

"Um . . . how?" Keith asked. "It looks very well-made."

"Yes," Mark agreed. "That's definitely high-quality craftsmanship."

"The robot guard!" Lulu yelled. "Use it to open the cell!"

Mark looked at the robot lying crumpled next to the empty cell Mercy had been locked in. "This robot?" he asked. "Looks broken."

"Totally," Keith agreed. "That is one broken robot."

Lulu could barely contain her impatience and anger. "Put the robot's face on the cell's scanner. It'll read the robot's eyes and open the door."

"Really?" Mark said. "That is high-tech!"

"JUST DO IT!" Lulu roared.

Working together, Mark and Keith managed to lift the robot's eyes up to the cell's scanner. CLANG! The locks disengaged, and the door sprung open. Lulu rushed out.

"Lulu!" Ace called from his cell. "Let us out!"

"Sorry," Lulu sneered. "Not part of the plan. I'm gonna rule the world, and NO ONE can stop me!"

"We'll stop you!" PB shouted.

Lulu laughed at the idea of the team taking her on. "Hilarious! You can't even get out! Maybe if Stuper-Dog there still had his powers . . . but I took them away, 'member? I'll say goodbye to Superman for you. Later, nerds!"

And with that, Lulu left, feeling positively triumphant. She was followed by Mark and Keith.

Back in his headquarters, Lex Luthor lounged in an office chair, gloating over the Super Heroes. "Well, well, well," he said. "If it isn't the Justice League. Captured by me. Entirely on my own."

Cyborg and Aquaman exchanged a doubtful look. They knew for a fact that Luthor hadn't caught them on his own. In fact, they weren't sure he'd had anything to do with it at all. It had been those blasted guinea pigs with their amazing powers.

"Let us out of here, Lex!" Superman demanded urgently.

"I could do that," Luthor said, pretending to consider the suggestion. "Or I could do this." He jumped up and did a triumphant dance. Reaching into his pockets, he pulled out confetti, threw it in the air, and danced like a football player who had just scored a touchdown.

"Uh, how long have you had that confetti in your pockets?" Wonder Woman asked.

"Too long," Luthor growled. "But the waiting's been totally worth it, because you losers are going down for good."

The clock Lulu had shown on her phone, counting down to her explosion, read fourteen minutes and forty-five seconds. . . .

WHAM! Krypto slammed his body into the cell's force-field door and crashed to the floor, hard. He repeatedly tried to break through the force field and failed every time.

"Okay, so what's the plan, Super-Dog?" Ace asked.

Krypto just lay on the floor in pain. "There isn't one."

Chip looked puzzled. "But there has to be some way we can—"

"No," Krypto barked, defeated. "It's too late."

PB looked determined. "Well, we can't just give up! Like the time The Cheetah had Wonder Woman trapped in her jungle lair—"

"PB," Krypto interrupted, "you're not Wonder Woman!"

PB looked hurt. Ace came to her defense. "Hey, hey, now," he said. "We've all been working our tails off here."

"And all that's done," Krypto argued, "is get me trapped while my best friend is in trouble!"

"Now, look," Ace said. "I know how much you're hurting, but that doesn't mean you can take it out on these guys. They're just trying to help."

Krypto thought a moment. Then he said, "You're right. It's not your fault. I mean, you're not . . ." He hesitated.

"Not what?" Merton asked.

21

Struggling to pick the right words, Krypto said, "You weren't built like me. So you can't be . . ."

"Just say it," Ace said. He had a pretty good idea of what Krypto was thinking about them.

"No . . . ," Krypto said.

"Say it," Ace demanded.

"You're not heroes," Krypto finally said.

Disappointed in Krypto, Ace just shook his head. "Well, if this is how a hero acts, then I'm glad I'm not one."

Krypto looked at PB, Merton, and Chip. "Your hearts are in the right place, but saving the world is tough." The three friends looked hurt. PB wiped away a tear.

"You don't know a thing about tough," Ace told Krypto accusingly. "You use us to get your owner back. And the second something goes wrong? You throw us away. Well, we may not be heroes, but you're not a real friend!"

That stung. "Oh, I'm not a real friend?" Krypto

snapped back. "You never liked me. You were just using me to get to your farm."

"Oh, come on!" Ace said. "You're so full of it!"

To a human, Krypto and Ace would have sounded like two angry dogs growling at each other. But their argument went on.

"Guess what?" Krypto said angrily. "I never wanted to be your friend, either. And if I hadn't lost my powers, we never would've even met!"

At that moment, Krypto noticed the other rescue pets staring at him with wide eyes. "What?" he asked. "What is it?"

"You're flying," Chip said, amazed.

"What?" Krypto exclaimed. He looked down. He was hovering above the floor. "My powers! I'm back!"

"The toy dinosaur has passed," Merton lowered his eyes and said solemnly.

With a rush of energy and confidence, Krypto lunged toward the door and smashed it open! CLANK! The force of his blow was so powerful that it knocked out all the force fields, releasing the other Super-Pets. They walked out of their cages, feeling awkward after everything Krypto had said. Ace avoided him completely.

As Krypto stretched and cracked his neck, PB asked, "So . . . what happens now?"

"I'm going to save Superman," Krypto said, his voice full of determination. "But don't worry," he added. "I'll still get you to your farm. That way we all get what we really wanted." He smacked the tag on his collar, releasing his cape and revealing the *S* on the tag. "Pup, pup, and away!" He sprang into the air and flew up through the roof of the prison.

PB took a step toward Ace. He was shaking his head, still angry at Krypto. "Ace," she said, "we've gotta help."

Ace stared at her. "Why should we? You heard the guy. He's better off without us."

Halfway up the towering LexCorp skyscraper, an outdoor deck featured trees, bushes, grass, benches, and statues. Upon arriving with her guinea pig army, Lulu spotted a gigantic statue of Lex Luthor. Using her Orange Kryptonite powers, she shook the statue on its base without even touching it!

Watching her work to topple the enormous statue with just her mind, Keith turned to Mark and observed, "I'm gonna go ahead and say I think she should go to therapy."

"I think so, too," Mark agreed, nodding. "I'm

hugely in favor of therapy. You know?"

"Of course," Keith said.

"You work out your body," Mark said. "Why wouldn't you work out your mind?"

"Exactly," Keith agreed.

Finally, the statue pitched forward, falling off the edge of the deck and plummeting toward the sidewalk many stories below. But then it froze in midair!

Krypto had caught the statue before it could hit the ground and hurt anyone.

"Ugh," Lulu groaned when she saw who had caught the statue. "This guy again?"

Overhead, Lois Lane rode in a news chopper to get video of the events for the evening broadcast. "Fly over there," she told the helicopter pilot, pointing to Lulu and her guinea pig army. "We're getting the shot."

Krypto set the colossal Lex Luthor statue down on the ground safely and then zipped up to the deck. THUMP! Landing in front of the guinea pig army with a thunderous bang, he clearly had all his strength back. The guinea pigs charged at him.

Nutmeg reached Krypto first. The Super-Dog easily tossed the mutant guinea pig aside.

Superpowered guinea pig after guinea pig came at Krypto, but they were no match for the Super-Dog.

Finally, a creature called Rainbow Guinea Pig trotted up to Krypto and blasted him with rainbows. The lovely rainbows didn't hurt him at all. As Krypto slowly walked toward her, she panicked and fled. "Even rainbows can't stop him!" she cried as she ran away.

Lulu's army had fallen to Krypto, but it had given Lulu the time she needed to make her way to Lex Luthor. . . .

22

Up on the top floor of the LexCorp Tower, Lex Luthor strutted in front of the captured Justice League Super Heroes, running a hand across their cells. Mercy looked on.

"Any last words?" he asked them, grinning at the thought of their utter defeat.

BOOM! Lulu blasted a hole in the wall and stomped into the room with Mark and Keith right behind her. "I have several words for you, Lex," she grumbled in her deep voice. "But I don't think you want to hear them."

Lulu grabbed the cowering Luthor, slid a cone-shaped dog collar around his neck, and tossed him into a cell.

Mercy quickly backed into an elevator and pressed a button. As the doors closed, she said, "I don't get paid enough for this."

SHHH-BAM! Steel doors closed, confining all the prisoners together. "Hey, guys, this is crazy, huh?" Luthor said to the Justice League Super Heroes in a weak effort to pretend they were on the same side. "We're all in here together. It's fun, right?"

Meanwhile, Lulu floated over to a control panel, joining Mark and Keith. "Are you sure about this?" Mark asked. She shoved them aside and was about to press a launch button, when a voice commanded, "Stand down!"

Lulu looked up from the control panel to see Krypto standing in a heroic pose. "Okay, Krypto," the power-mad guinea pig sighed. "You are definitely stalking me now. I'm, like, creeped out. Bye!" As she lowered her claw toward the button, Krypto smashed into her, tackling her away from the control panel and all the way out of the building. Holding her, he hovered in midair a short distance away from the tower.

"Where is Superman?" he demanded.

"You're too late," Lulu told him. "I'm sending him back to the place from whence he came!" With a flick of her pinky claw, she used her power to activate the launch button back in Luthor's office.

CLICK.

23

RUMBLE! Krypto looked back at LexCorp Tower and saw the entire skyscraper shaking. Inside, Lex Luthor and the Justice League Super Heroes were being tumbled like socks in a clothes dryer.

"What's happening?" Superman shouted.

"Oh, yeah, funny story," Luthor said. "I turned my office into a rocket ship." The Super Heroes looked at him like he'd lost his evil mind. "What?" he asked. "All the billionaires have rocket ships!"

"It's true." Batman, who was secretly billionaire Bruce Wayne, confirmed.

As Krypto stared at the trembling building, Lulu slipped out of his grasp. Suddenly, the roof ripped off the top of the tower and the top floors slowly started to lift into the sky, sheathed in metal. FROOOOOM!

Smoke billowed out of the base of the rocket ship and onto the landscaped deck below. Krypto zoomed down to see if everyone there was all right. When he landed on the deck, he saw Mark and Keith crawling out of the smoke, coughing.

"What's going on?" Krypto demanded.

"The Justice League guys and Baldie are in the rocket," Mark explained. "Lulu launched it. She definitely needs therapy. To be honest, we're seriously starting to regret helping her."

"If the rocket ship reaches the stratosphere," Keith added, "it'll implode. GO!"

Krypto didn't need to hear any more. He flew into the air, chasing the rocket like a gigantic stick someone had tossed for him to fetch. "I'm coming for you, Superman!"

But suddenly Lulu was there. She grabbed Krypto. "Not so fast!"

"Hey, hamster!" Lois called from the nearby helicopter, taking off her shoe. "That's my dog! Kinda! Future step-dog!" Lois hurled her shoe at Lulu, beaning her right in the eye! Startled, Lulu let go of Krypto and turned to deal with the furious reporter. "You should've stayed in your lane, Lois!" Lulu told her.

Using her powers, Lulu trapped the helicopter in her long-distance grasp. Then she turned to Krypto. "Who will you save, doggy?" she sneered. "The man you love or the woman he does?" She abruptly chopped her paw through the air. Her gesture sent the chopper and Lois plummeting toward a nearby building.

Krypto didn't know what to do. He couldn't save them both!

But suddenly, the Super-Pets appeared by his side.

"You came back for me," Krypto said, awed.

"You know what they say about dogs," Ace said. "We love unconditionally."

Krypto was humbled. His friends had forgiven him and were there to help. Speaking of help—

"You save Superman!" Krypto shouted to his fellow Super-Pets.

"But . . . ," Ace protested, not sure how to stop a rocket.

"I trust you!" Krypto shouted as he dove, zooming down toward the falling helicopter with Lois in it.

The shelter animals looked at each other. "He trusts us," Merton said in disbelief. "To save them from a rocket. Us."

"Do we trust him to trust us?" Chip rubbed wrung his paws and asked nervously.

PB gestured toward her back. "Hop on, y'all. 'Cause this pig's about to go HAM." Ace, Chip, and Merton quickly clambered onto her back. PB started to grow, expanding into the air after the rising rocket as fast as she could. Merton screamed, holding on for dear life.

Meanwhile, Lois and the pilot and the helicopter were descending rapidly, drawing closer and closer to the building below them. Krypto raced after her. Lulu tried to throw obstacles in his way, tearing buildings apart with her power and sending huge chunks flying into his path. But he ducked, dodged, and used his heat vision to blast debris out of his way.

The chopper was about to crash into the roof of the building, when . . . it stopped! Lois looked out and saw Krypto holding the helicopter, stopping it inches from impact. She and the pilot jumped out of the chopper and landed safely on the roof.

Watching Krypto foil her evil plan—again—made Lulu angrier than ever!

PB had grown into the sky almost as high as the rising rocket ship, but not quite. "I can't reach!" she said in a strained voice. "This is as big as I can get!"

Ace yanked Chip onto his back. Facing forward, he called out, "Merton, hit it!" The old turtle ran down to the base of PB's tail and then zipped back toward Ace and Chip at top speed, using her shell to launch them off PB and into the air. With Chip riding Ace like a rodeo cowboy on a bucking bronco, they zoomed up to the rocket ship and landed on it. Chip turned around and looked at Merton and PB receding in the distance below them.

High above Earth on Luthor's rocket, Ace turned to Chip and said, "You're up, kid. Use your power to open this ship up like a can of tuna."

Chip nodded his head rapidly. "You've got this, Chip," he told himself. "Take a risk." Using his electricity like a saw, he cut through the metal base of the rocket.

Inside, the rocket rumbled. The Justice League Super Heroes looked concerned.

Outside, Chip kept sawing away. But the ship shook, knocking him off-balance. He accidentally hit one of the ship's engines with his lightning bolt. BOOM! The engine exploded, knocking Chip off the rocket!

As he fell, he screamed, but—

FLOMP! Chip landed right in PB's arms. She shrank back down to normal size with Merton next to her. "Whew," Chip sighed. "Now it's up to Ace."

Up on the rocket, Ace saw a panel warning that the rocket was near the stratosphere and about to implode. In the flashing red light of the warning panel, Ace ripped through the last ribbon of metal. He did it!

The base separated from the cylindrical body of the rocket, and everyone fell out, still trapped in their containment units, plummeting toward Earth! As they hurtled downward, the rocket above them imploded. BOOOOM! The Super-Pets had gotten them out just in time!

24

Back down in Metropolis, Lulu faced off against Krypto. They battled.

Krypto shouted, "It's over, hamster!"

"Hamster?" Lulu bellowed. "I AM NOT A HAMSTER!"

Just as Krypto threw Lulu into a building, defeating her, he spotted Superman and the rest of the League of Justice plummeting toward the ground. "NO!" he cried.

But there was no need to worry. Once again, PB grew to her giant state and caught them like a huge, comfy cushion in middle of Daily Square Park.

Krypto flew down to join his friends.

"Did you see that?" Chip said excitedly.

"We all used our powers, like a bunch of real Super Heroes!" Ace said.

"It's not superpowers that make you a hero," Krypto said, suddenly realizing something.

"Then what does?" asked PB.

"I'm looking at it," Krypto said, staring straight into the other dog's eyes.

Krypto turned Ace's bandanna around, and it caught the wind like a cape. The Super-Pets grinned. They were heroes!

"Time to join our fellow Super Heroes!" Krypto added. "Let's get them out!"

They zipped over to help the members of the Justice League. When Superman saw Krypto, he lit up. "That's my dog!" he said. "I missed you, buddy!"

Playing it cool, Krypto barked, "I may have thought about you from time to time." But then he dropped his cool, rushed to free his person, and rolled onto his back for some super belly rubs.

"So, what do you say?" Superman asked. "Should we watch the baking show tonight?"

"Oh, yeah!" Krypto said. He noticed Lois running toward them. "And why don't you bring her?"

Hugging Superman and Krypto, Lois said, "I'm so happy you're all right!" Then she whipped out her phone to record an exclusive interview about the day's events. "Tell me everything."

Freeing Green Lantern, Chip lost his balance and fell into her arms.

"Don't worry," Green Lantern reassured him. "I got you." Chip beamed at her, finally feeling safe!

Merton and The Flash high-fived each other in slow motion.

"Okay," Merton said. "What's happening?"

"Wow," The Flash said. "This is so weird."

"So beautiful," Merton observed.

"High-fiving so slow when we're both really fast," The Flash said, amazed.

PB shyly approached her hero, Wonder Woman. "Princess Diana of Themyscira, Daughter of Hippolyta, Protector of the Amazons, I humbly present myself, Super Hog—still brainstorming my hero name—to you." She unlocked the door.

Wonder Woman stepped out, lifted PB into the air, and held her close. "You'll be a mighty warrior!" she told the delighted potbellied pig. "And cuddle buddy!"

Aquaman was still locked in his tank. "Woe is me," he sighed. "No one cares about the water guy." But then Keith, no longer icy, unlocked the tank, freeing Aquaman.

"Man," said Keith, "I'm literally the water guy!"

Aquaman hugged the guinea pig, who kissed him.

"Little piggy kisses," Aquaman said happily.

Mark had already freed Cyborg, who asked, "Need a light?" He reignited Mark with his arm cannon. Mark leapt into Cyborg's arms, crying, "Look at me! Oh, thank you!"

Ace freed Batman. They exchanged an awkward look.

"So," Batman said. "You are a dog. I am the Batman. Sorry, I'm not really great with animals."

"Yeah, I'm not really great with people," Ace said. "Probably because of my traumatic puppyhood."

"When I was a child," Batman said, "my family was taken from me."

"When I was a puppy," Ace replied, "I was taken from my family."

"So I've steeled myself," Batman explained.

"I always keep my emotions in check," Ace said.

They both said at the same time, "No one ever gets past my impenetrable defenses."

Then Ace looked at Batman. "Ah, what the heck," he said, leaping at Batman and licking his face.

At first Batman resisted, but then he gave in, laughing. "Good boy," he said. "Okay, the Batman loves you, too."

Superman was scratching Krypto behind the ears. "So, buddy," he said, "looks like you made friends."

"Yup!" Krypto affirmed. "And now I've got to bring them to Smallville. I promised them that it would be their new—"

As he was speaking, Krypto saw his friends with their new perfect matches: Chip with Green Lantern, PB with Wonder Woman, Merton with The Flash, and Ace with Batman.

"—home," he said, trailing off.

From his cell, Lex Luthor called out, "Hello? Excuse me. Is anyone going to let me out? Perhaps a cute little kitten?"

"No!" said Whiskers, walking past.

But Lulu wasn't done yet.

When she saw all the Super-Pets looking happy with their new Justice League friends, she felt rage boiling inside her. She decided to POWER UP.

Pulling the Orange Kryptonite fragment from underneath the scrap of Superman's cape that she'd tied around her neck, Lulu broke it into pieces and absorbed the shards into her head! Glowing orange, she grew. A crackling bubble of destructive energy surrounded her.

"Uh-oh," Merton said when she saw Lulu in her terrifying new form.

Immediately, the new Super Hero and Super-Pet pairs flew into action, battling Lulu together. Chip fought with Green Lantern. PB joyfully battled with Wonder Woman. Merton combined her speed with The Flash's. Ace synchronized perfectly with Batman's attack. And as always, Krypto fought alongside Superman.

But Lulu was just too strong for them. They couldn't penetrate her orange energy shield. Laughing a monstrous laugh, Lulu trapped Superman against a building with chunks of fallen debris.

Krypto knew what he had to do. There was only one way to stop Lulu—the Solar Paw Punch! Flying high into the sky to be bathed in the sun's rays, he felt himself more energized than ever. The effects of the Green Kryptonite had worn off completely.

Krypto flew faster than he had ever flown before and rammed Lulu's force field. His Solar Paw Punch shattered Lulu's orange rage bubble! The shock wave caused the shards of Orange Kryptonite in her body to crumble and turn to dust.

"NOOO!" Lulu shrieked as she felt her powers fade away. Now, unable to resist gravity, she fell out of the sky, and landed in the hot water on a hot dog cart on the street below. SPLASH!

"What have you done to me?" she squeaked. "I'm in hot dog water, aren't I?" She looked up and saw Krypto using his heat vision to seal her in the water chamber. "NOOO!" she screamed again as she swam around.

Krypto hurried to save Superman from the pile of rubble.

"What a good dog," Superman said gratefully. Krypto wagged his tail.

25

Lulu, trapped in the hot dog water, heard an electric buzzing. Someone was using a laser to open the lid Krypto had sealed with his heat vision! "Could it be . . . Lex?" she thought hopefully, ready to forgive him again.

The lid opened, and she saw Mercy wearing Lex's mechanical power suit.

"Oh, it's you," Lulu said, disappointed. "Hi."

"Let's be honest," Mercy said. "The two of us are the real brains behind this operation. Forget Lex—we should team up." She extended her hand to Lulu. "So, what do you say? You wanna come live in a studio apartment?"

"Like . . . with you? Like, a pet-owner situation?" Lulu said. "Hmm, let me think— Yes, yes, the answer is yes!"

Mercy scooped her up and they flew off together, thanks to the power suit.

As they flew, Lulu said, "So, something to know

about me—I like chin scratchies, and there's a spot on my back that makes my leg kick."

A few days later, Krypto happily flew through Metropolis and landed next to PB in a park for a planned meeting. "Nice costume, PB!" he told her, admiring her new superhero outfit.

"Thanks!" she said. "It even has magnets!" She showed off her magnetic bracelets, clinking them together just like Wonder Woman. Thanks to the magnets, she could mimic Wonder Woman's signature move even with her short arms!

Chip floated down in a Green Lantern energy orb.

"Hey, Chiptonite!" Krypto greeted him. "How's it going with Jessica?"

"We're getting pretty close as person and pet," Chip reported cheerfully. "She even put a ring on it." He held up his paw, showing off a tiny lantern ring like Green Lantern's.

WHOOSH! Merton raced up to the other three wearing a red superhero costume like The Flash's. "How long is this gonna take?" she asked. "I've got a hot date with two firefighter helmets. Spoiler alert: they're twins."

SCREECH! The Batmobile raced around a corner. Wearing a bat-hound costume, Ace stuck his head out the window, enjoying the breeze with his tongue flapping. When Batman stopped at a red light, Ace barked and Batman patted him, giving him permission to jump out. Ace leapt out the window and shot a bat-winged grappling hook from his collar. He swung across traffic and landed dramatically next to the others, striking a heroic pose.

"Right on time, brother," Krypto said.

"So, what's the mission?" Ace asked, getting right to business.

Keith and Mark popped up out of a manhole. "Our intel indicates that a dog has been mutated," Mark reported. "It could be dangerous."

"We have to stop him!" Keith said.

"Tighten your collars," Krypto told everybody. "We've got work to do!"

In another part of the city, a giant glowing blue corgi with red eyes smashed cars like they were toys, roaring and shooting out tentacles of energy!

"Super-Pets, activate!" Krypto barked.

They flew into action, ready to take on the mutant corgi!

THE SUPER-PETS WERE ON THE JOB!